"Take off your shoes."

Her cheeks warmed. "It's not proper. What kind of example would I set for Hannah if I did that?"

"You're ruining them. Besides, I expect a healthy dose of common sense to go along with Hannah's education."

"But—" she said weakly, and then sighed. Why argue? He was right.

She motioned Stuart to turn his back, then sat down on a nearby boulder and removed her shoes and stockings. When she glanced up and caught him spying, she stood abruptly, letting her dress rustle into place.

He ignored her discomfort and stared at her feet. Then slowly his gaze moved up the length of her to her face, leaving behind a trail of tingles. "It has been a long time since I walked barefoot with a beautiful girl."

* * *

The Angel and the Outlaw
Harlequin® Historical #876—December 2007

Dear Reader,

The idea for this story came to me on one of my visits to the Old Point Loma Lighthouse in San Diego and the nearby tide pools. Inspired by the beauty and ruggedness of the terrain, the tales of shipwrecks off the coast, the whaling station nearby and the last of the California bandits, I wondered what type of man would choose to live such an isolated life.

It seemed that a stubborn man like Stuart, who is running from the law and in need of redemption, could use a little help from a feisty woman to make peace with his past. Rachel, with her tough life in the backcountry mining camps, is not the type to shy away from a challenge.

This is my first published book, and I would love to hear from my readers. You can reach me at P.O. Box 606, Rockton, IL 61072 or contact me through my Web site at www.kathrynleighalbright.com.

I hope you enjoy *The Angel and the Outlaw*!

Kathryn

KATHRYN ALBRIGHT

The ANGEL and the OUTLAW

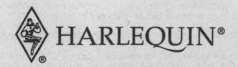

HARLEQUIN®

TORONTO • NEW YORK • LONDON
AMSTERDAM • PARIS • SYDNEY • HAMBURG
STOCKHOLM • ATHENS • TOKYO • MILAN • MADRID
PRAGUE • WARSAW • BUDAPEST • AUCKLAND

ISBN-13: 978-0-373-29476-3
ISBN-10:   0-373-29476-X

THE ANGEL AND THE OUTLAW

www.eHarlequin.com

Printed in U.S.A.

To my mother and father, who taught me
to go after my dreams.

Thank you for your love, support and encouragement.

Prologue

San Francisco, California, 1870

At the sound of someone running up his ship's gangplank, Matthew Taylor looked up from the scatter of charts on his desk.

"Matthew! Let me in! I must speak with you."

He strode to the door and stopped short at the sight before him. "Linnea!"

The light from the cabin's oil lamp exposed harsh bruises against the pale skin on her face. Blood dripped from a cracked lip. Under the dark hooded cloak, her blond hair, usually swept up in the latest fashion, hung unkempt to her shoulders.

"My God! What happened?"

"I...I killed John!" she gasped. "He was going after Hannah."

Suddenly he realized the bundle she held was her daughter. "Let me take her." He pulled the cover away, breathing a sigh of relief that Hannah was free of any sign of battering. She was shaking, just as her mother was. He laid her on his bunk and turned back to Linnea. "Tell me what happened," he said, the rage in his voice barely subdued.

Her eyes filled with tears. "I… Might I use your handkerchief?"

He handed one to her. God, he couldn't stand the tears. "Don't cry, Linnea. You know I'll help."

"Yes," she said softly. "I know."

With his fingers under her chin, he lifted her face to the light. "How long has this been going on?"

She turned away from him. "Awhile."

He poured a brace of whiskey into his mug and handed it to her. "It's all I have."

"Taylor!" John Newcomb bellowed from outside.

Linnea's eyes widened. "I thought he was dead!"

"Taylor!" John was closer now. "You holing up with my wife? You send her on out here. We've got unfinished business."

Linnea started to rise.

"No," Matthew said, and motioned for her to stay put.

She grasped his arm. "Matthew. Be careful. He's changed since you last saw him."

He stared at her, taking in the changes the past few years had wrought on her. A hundred things went through his head in that moment, none of which he could say to her as a married woman. *Why did you marry this animal? Why didn't you wait for me?* He sighed. At the least, he could protect her.

He squeezed her hand. "I'll just talk to him. I don't

want a fight, but I won't run from one, either." He reached into a desk drawer and drew out his Colt .44.

On the wharf, John Newcomb leaned heavily against the railing, his tie askew against his linen shirt. "Send my wife out, Taylor. She don't belong with you."

"You're drunk, Mr. Newcomb. Go home and sleep it off."

"I'm not leaving without my girls. Linnea! We need to talk. I…at least give me a chance to apologize."

Matthew heard the door creak behind him.

"Go away," Linnea said softly, her body half-hidden behind the door post. "We'll talk later."

"We'll talk now," John growled, and started up the gangplank, clutching his chest. "Then I'll have words with Taylor, here." Suddenly he stopped and leaned awkwardly on the ship's railing. As he straightened, he pulled a gun from his belt and aimed past Matthew.

A shot rang out.

"Mama!" Hannah screamed.

Matthew watched in horror as Linnea crumpled to her knees, a look of stunned surprise on her face.

John stormed up the gangplank, aiming his gun for a second shot at her. "I'll teach you to at shoot me."

"No!" Matthew roared. He whipped up his Colt and squeezed the trigger.

In the loud report of the gun, John Newcomb staggered, but then regained his footing. He swung his gun toward Matthew. "You can't have her, Taylor. I'll kill you both before I let that happen."

Matthew steadied his gun, aimed at Newcomb's chest and fired.

Newcomb fell forward hard, landing with a heavy thud. The wharf's gas lamp cast a yellow light over the blood saturating his shirt and dripping onto the wooden planks beneath him.

Matthew threw down his gun and hurried to Linnea. Blood trickled across her forehead. She was so still, so pale. Crouching, he gathered her in his arms, unable to breathe, afraid she was hurt or—worse—dead.

Her large gray eyes fluttered open. "I'm all right."

His heart pounded in his chest.

She raised her hand to his cheek, the worry in her eyes for him now. "Matthew, I'm all right."

He let out a long, shuddering breath. "I thought…"

"Yes. I know."

He hugged her to him, burying his face in her neck until his heartbeat slowed to normal. He couldn't bear to lose her.

After a moment she struggled up on her elbows. "Is he dead?"

Matthew followed her gaze. He walked over to the still form. Not breathing. He rolled Newcomb over to his back and felt for a pulse at his throat.

Nothing.

"What happens now?" Linnea asked, her voice shaking. "Should we contact the authorities?"

Chapter One

Southern California, 1873

Stuart Taylor crouched on a flat boulder and pulled his trap up from the harbor floor. A small brown lobster slid to the corner of the crate. He grabbed it, turning it over to make sure of its size, and then tossed it back into the water. "Come back when you've grown," he murmured. Then, placing new bait in the trap, he stood and swung the trap out as far as possible, releasing the hemp rope at the last second. The crate splashed into the brine and sank quickly beyond sight.

He looked for his other lobster trap, but it was gone—rope and all. Someone was still stealing from him. He'd warned off two boys a few days ago with a bullet into their boat. Their sudden departure had convinced him they wouldn't try again. Maybe he'd been wrong.

Great. Guess he and Hannah would be eating beans

tonight. Not the best way to celebrate a birthday. He grabbed the bucket at his feet and made his way up the narrow dirt path.

Hannah stood at the stone doorstep, anxiety filling her heart-shaped face until she caught sight of him. She wore her one good dress, the dark-chocolate-brown one he'd laid out last night. A white pinafore covered it, wrinkled in one spot now where her hands had twisted and worried the fabric. Uncanny how that trait of her mother's manifested itself in Hannah, though she'd only been three when Linnea died.

"Did you eat?"

She nodded, and with the bob of her head, he spied her tangled mass of blond hair. "Forgot something, birthday girl," he said gruffly, turning her toward the kitchen. "You can't go into town looking like something washed in by the waves."

She crossed her arms over her chest and stood stiffly while he brushed her hair then tied it in a ponytail with an old blue ribbon. The face that stared back at him grew more like her mother's every day. The dove-gray eyes shone with anticipation for the promised trip. She was lonely here. So lonely the thought of a trip into town had her flushed with excitement and up before dawn. He felt it, too—the isolation, the quiet. But it was safe.

He followed Hannah outside and boosted her onto his horse, Blanco. She fidgeted, patting the dusty animal on its withers. He grabbed the lead rope. "See that you don't wiggle right off your perch."

They took the trail that led from the tip of the windy

peninsula, four hundred feet above sea level, to the small town on the water's edge. He didn't get into town much, only when supplies ran low, but today was August 10, Hannah's birthday, and he wanted to make it special for her.

He drew closer to La Playa and his anxiety increased in measure. Surely the risk of discovery had diminished now. It had been more than three years since the accident. Hannah didn't even look the same. She had stretched up into a thin wisp of a girl who seldom stood still. Her naturally pale skin had taken on a golden glow over the long summer days.

He rubbed his smooth chin, remembering the dark beard and mustache that once covered his face. He didn't look the same either. Still, doubts niggled at his mind. Dorian wasn't stupid, and he wasn't a quitter. San Francisco might be five hundred miles away but sooner or later Dorian would find him—and if Dorian found him, so would the law. Perhaps he should think about moving on.

Halfway to town, the trail sloped steeply through a brush-studded canyon. Two small lizards scurried from under the horse's shadow and dashed into the nearby chaparral as he led Blanco around one last sandstone curve. The harbor opened up before them, deep blue and sparkling in the sunlight. Barely visible through the scruffy bushes to the south lay the whaling port. He raised his face to the wind and sniffed. "Smell that, Hannah? Just salt and sage. No whale butchered today."

Turning toward La Playa, he led Blanco past a steamer moored at the new wharf before heading up

San Antonio Street and past the Mexican Government Custom House. A few odd-shaped buildings, some built of wood and some of adobe, hugged each side of the square like ticks on the ears of a short-haired dog.

Stuart stopped at the community well and filled his canteens, all the while taking in the surrounding sounds the way a deaf man would who for one day is able to hear. Loud clanging rang out from the livery's half-opened doorway as the blacksmith forged a new tool or horseshoe. A thin, aproned woman swept the front boardwalk of the town's only mercantile.

Hannah tugged on his shirt.

"All right, all right. I'm going."

Looping the two canteens over the saddle horn, he walked back to Morley's Mercantile. Two young women stood at the opened doorway of the store, giggling and whispering behind gloved hands. He glanced up while tying the reins on the hitching rail. Both attractive, especially the blonde. He turned back to help Hannah.

"There on his forehead. Do you see it?"

He slowed in the act of setting Hannah on the ground. So he was to supply their gossip for today. He clenched his hands. He'd hate to disappoint them. Straightening, he leveled his gaze at the two.

The blonde quieted. She must be the banker's wife—or daughter. Her dress was quality through and through, right down to her matching green parasol. He hadn't seen anything so fancy since he'd left San Francisco. Her eyes judged him coolly before she whirled about with a toss of her head and entered the store.

Anger surged through him. Already he could feel people staring at him through the streaked windowpanes. He couldn't care less that they talked about him. But Hannah—Hannah, he worried about. She might not talk anymore, but she could hear just fine. He'd rather take her anywhere than into the store right now.

But it was her birthday. And he'd promised this trip for weeks.

He grasped her hand and helped her jump onto the boardwalk before stepping up himself.

The other woman, the one who'd gotten an earful, remained standing in the doorway, curiosity etched in her strong face. He wouldn't call her pretty—yet the sum of her features pulled together in a pleasant way. She wore a plain yellow dress, simple and sturdy, and a straw hat that covered thick auburn hair.

He stepped close—closer than was conventional—and dragged off his seaman's cap, giving her a good view of his scar. He met her unflinching gaze full-on—challenging her to speak. She was older than he'd first thought. Fine lines splayed from the corners of her eyes and her nose was sunburned and peeling. He let his gaze wander the length of her until he arrived again at her face, and found himself slightly irritated for enjoying the trip. "By all means, believe everything you hear."

Her cheeks flamed scarlet. With an almost imperceptible nod of her head—or was it actually a raising of her chin?—she stepped aside for him to enter the building.

The scent of cloves and cinnamon intermingled with the barrel of pears in the doorway. He breathed deeply and tried to shake off the discontent he felt. This was Hannah's birthday trip, and by God he'd make it special.

The blonde stood at the counter speaking with the lanky owner of the mercantile and glancing over her shoulder at Stuart every few seconds. Terrance Morley drummed his fingers on the countertop. "Mornin', Taylor. Things quiet up your way?"

Stuart hesitated a fraction of a second and then nodded. Things were always quiet at the lighthouse. He handed Morley the list of needed supplies.

Suddenly, Hannah let go of his hand and dashed across the room. Stuart followed slowly, a sinking sensation in his stomach. He hated to put a damper on her fascination with the trinkets and products, but whatever the item might be, likely they couldn't afford it. He'd planned only to buy her six sarsaparilla candy sticks, one for each of her six years, and a new hair ribbon.

She spun around holding a new doll with shiny waves of painted black hair and red lips. She fingered the doll's pretty green dress and ruffled underthings. He knew what would come next and steeled himself against the disappointment that would transform her face. Before the accident he wouldn't have thought twice about the cost of the doll. Although not rich, he had been comfortable, and the future held such promise. But now, on a light keeper's salary, the toy cost more than he could afford.

The woman in yellow entered the store, the sun casting her shadow across the hardwood floor. Morley glanced up, started to greet her and spied Hannah holding the doll.

"Put that down!" he shouted.

Startled, Hannah jumped. The doll crashed to the floor, its china head shattering at her feet. She stared in frozen shock at the pieces.

"Now look what you've done!" Morley yelled and pointed a bony finger at the mess. He charged around the end of the counter and jabbed Hannah's shoulder. "Children have no business being in here without proper supervision. You'll pay for that, missy."

Stuart leveled his gaze. "That's enough, Morley."

Tears brimmed in Hannah's eyes. She was scared— and sorry—even though the words wouldn't come. Stuart put his hand on her shoulder. "It was an accident, Hannah."

Next to him, the blonde turned on Hannah. "You must apologize to Mr. Morley this instant, child."

"I said that's enough," Stuart said, making sure there was no mistaking the warning in his voice. "And I'll thank you to keep to your own business, ma'am."

She glared at him, obviously perceiving the double meaning of his words, then stuck her nose higher in the air and walked from the store.

Slowly Hannah stooped and picked up the fragments of china.

I should scold her, Stuart told himself, but Mr. Morley had done a strong job of that. "Hannah," he said, sharper than he intended.

She stopped her gathering and glanced up, the tears spilling onto her cheeks in earnest now. Tightness wrapped around his chest and squeezed at the sight of her misery. Linnea would have handled this differently. He gentled his tone. "Put those on the counter and wait outside."

When she had done as he asked, he stepped up to the counter. He would settle the cost of the toy, but he'd have to omit an item or two from his list. How could he salvage her birthday after this?

The woman in yellow stooped to pick up one last fragment of china and the body of the doll. She placed them next to his parcels.

"Miss Houston, you don't need to clean up," the clerk said. "You'll cut yourself."

"You frightened the girl."

Her reproachful voice held a hint of soft Midwestern twang.

"She should sweep the entire floor for her punishment," Morley said.

Stuart pressed his lips together, checking his urge to hit the man. "I'll take care of my girl. You just mind your store." He looked over his stack of supplies and removed the canned beef and fresh bread. He could hunt rabbits and quail as usual. And there was always fish. They'd make do with the tin of crackers. It would last longer than the bread, anyway. Stubbornly, he kept the six candy sticks. "Now what is my total with the doll?"

While Morley tallied the order, Stuart found himself watching the woman, surprised she had spoken in Hannah's defense—and a little suspicious, too. She strolled to the yard goods, smoothing her hand across one piece of fabric and then another.

She must have felt him staring. After a glance in his

direction she looked away, but her cheeks flushed pink. She selected two bundles of yarn and set them on the far end of the counter. The scent of honeysuckle wafted over him, feminine, inviting. How long had it been since he smelled anything other than the brine of the ocean?

"You aren't charging full price for the doll, are you Terrance?" she asked.

Mr. Morley stopped his tallying and frowned over his glasses at her.

"Part of the fault lies with you," she continued.

"That doesn't excuse the cost."

"But you startled the girl. If you'd asked her to put the doll down rather than speaking so sharply, she wouldn't have dropped it."

Morley caught Stuart's gaze. "Three dollars, Taylor."

The clerk's attitude disgusted him. The sooner Stuart got out of here, the better. He counted out the money and dropped it on the counter then picked up the box of supplies. The doll he left behind purposely. To have what was left of it would only distress Hannah.

He packed his saddlebags, and then helped Hannah onto Blanco. Despair knifed through him at the silent shaking of her shoulders. She had dressed so carefully this morning, had been so excited about this trip into town, and it had ended in a nightmare. Stuart's stomach knotted. He couldn't do anything about other people. They were cruel. Hell, life was cruel, but somehow he'd make it up to her.

A flash of yellow in the doorway caught his eye. He glanced up to see the woman watching him. He didn't quite know what to make of her. In the end she'd been kind, and so he tipped his cap to her.

She acknowledged him with a nod, her gaze steady.

Anxious to put the town and its people behind him, he led Blanco home. The bustling sounds of the harbor grated on his ears. The silence that shrouded them daily at the lighthouse would be safe—safe for him and safe for Hannah. No one and nothing would bother them… nothing but the never-ending quiet.

"Your yarn, Miss Houston." Terrance Morley leaned on the wooden counter and smiled—a smile Rachel could easily mistake for a leer if she gave room to the thought.

"Thank you, Mr. Morley."

"It was Terrance a moment ago."

"Yes, well. It was a bit presumptuous of me."

"But you've been coming in here for over two months now. I'd like you to use my given name."

"Oh," she said, not particularly thrilled with what others might read into the familiarity. "I'm a little uncomfortable with that." Her position as the new schoolteacher in this small town hinged on the degree of respectability she could maintain. At her interview with the school board she had downplayed the last few years she'd spent at the mining camp where coarseness and crudeness frequently overpowered a gentler nature. Instead, she had reframed the questions to answer them from her earlier life when she'd helped at the one-room schoolhouse in Wisconsin.

She picked up the yarn and turned to go, but stopped when she saw the broken doll. The head was shattered.

No amount of gluing could repair it. Fingering the mint-green satin dress and miniature crinoline, she thought of the girl's sad face. The wrinkled, too-small dress, the small hole in one stocking below the knee, all spoke of a girl with no mother to do for her. Rachel knew what it was like to live without a mother. At least she'd been lucky to have known hers for the first fourteen years of her life. How lonely the girl must be on the peninsula with no one but her father.

Since she'd moved to town two months ago, she'd heard stories of him. How he kept to himself and was unfriendly toward the townspeople. She didn't know what to believe and most likely shouldn't listen to half of it.

Still, she'd expected someone much older to be the town's enigma—someone grizzled, with bushy brows and an irascible nature. At most, Taylor must be all of thirty years—or perhaps thirty-five—for he had the solid, filled-out look of a man. His clothes were simple, serviceable—a faded blue chambray shirt, slightly snug across the stretch of his shoulders, tucked into canvas pants, and scruffy boots that passed for comfortable on his feet. A thick wisp of dark-brown hair fell across his temple and had obscured his scar until he purposely exposed it for her.

It was a hideous scar—puckered and red. She wondered how he'd really gotten it. Amanda said he'd been struck with a red-hot fire poker when he escaped from prison. That was ridiculous, of course. The lighthouse board would never have hired a convict. Since coming to town two months ago, Rachel had heard other stories about him as well, enough to know that no one knew anything definite about him at all.

Besides, it wasn't the scar that drew her, but the intensity of his blue gaze. When he'd stopped no more than a foot from her in the doorway she'd scarcely been able to breathe.

No, he wasn't her idea of a light keeper at all.

Chapter Two

Rachel jerked open the oven door and pulled out the roast.

Finished. Except for the gravy. Lamb wasn't her favorite dish, but she couldn't very well serve rabbit or fish tonight—not with company coming.

Reverend and Emma Crouse rented two rooms to Rachel and her brother, Caleb, on the condition that they would help with odd jobs around the place. That usually meant cooking for Rachel, and tending the horse and small carriage house for Caleb. Of course, four dollars a month from Rachel's teaching salary also helped cover their rent. Reverend and Emma Crouse were in their late sixties and ready to slow down a little. Staying with such an upstanding couple had helped with her acceptance into the community. One couldn't be too careful that way, especially after the years she'd lived in the mining camp. The roughness of the camp had rubbed off on her and try as she might to put it all behind her, unfortunate things would spring out of her mouth—or show up in her actions.

She pushed a strand of damp hair from her forehead, then leaned across the small table to open the window. A cool evening breeze swirled in heavy with the scent of brine from the ocean. Looking out into the early evening, she wondered what the light keeper and his daughter would be eating tonight. The two had been in her thoughts throughout the day, popping in unexpectedly.

She hadn't liked Amanda's attitude or Terrance Morley's for that matter. Maybe what they said about the light keeper was true. Perhaps he was a criminal. But even so, the girl—Hannah, he'd called her—should not be condemned along with the father. The man obviously cared for his daughter or he wouldn't have protected her from Terrance's tirade. There must be something good in him.

The kitchen door opened and Reverend Crouse entered. It seemed the room warmed as much from the heat that emanated from him as it did from the stove. "Supper ready?"

"Nearly." Then, knowing his next question, she answered, "Mrs. Crouse is in the parlor with the guests."

"Ah. Then I'd best get out there and greet them, too. Are you doing all right in here without Emma's help?" She nearly smiled at the relief on his face at her quick nod. Then he headed to the front of the parsonage.

Suddenly the back door crashed open and her brother barreled into the kitchen along with his dog. At fifteen, Caleb was neither a boy any longer, nor yet a man. Clumsy was what he was. He was growing so fast—already four inches taller than she. He reached for a dinner roll, and she caught the bony knob of his wrist just in time.

"Not before supper. Now take Settie right back outside."

He ignored her. "She's getting close, don't you think?"

Rachel studied the large black animal. The dog's bulging abdomen swayed as she walked around the small kitchen sniffing the different aromas. "Any day now, I suspect. She is so big I don't know how she manages to move."

"Enrique said he'll take a male. He thinks it might make a good hunter."

She frowned. Caleb could use a good friend, but someone other than Enrique. Together, the two of them got into too much mischief. She turned back to her preparations. "Well, for now Settie goes outside. Wash up. The food is ready."

Behind her, she heard Caleb maneuver the dog out the back door. When he didn't come right back in, she glanced through the window. He stood in the yard talking with Enrique and another boy. The way they leaned toward each other, whispering, unsettled her. She watched a moment longer and then tried to shake off her misgivings. Time to get supper on.

She carried a platter with the roast lamb surrounded by new potatoes to the dining table. When they were all seated, Rachel sat down across from Terrance

Morley and his sister, Elizabeth. The bouquet of roses he'd brought graced the center of the table, their delicate fragrance completely overwhelmed by the odor of mutton.

"Where's Caleb?" Emma Crouse asked.

"He's just outside with a friend. He'll be in shortly," Rachel said. "Perhaps we should go ahead before the food cools."

The reverend frowned, but bowed his head to say the blessing. Then the dishes were passed around and the talk turned to local business and how New San Diego was quickly becoming a ghost town. Rachel tried, but she just couldn't follow the conversation.

"If you'll excuse me a moment," She said, standing. "I'll just see what is keeping Caleb." Rachel walked into the kitchen and peered out the window into the empty yard. A feeling of foreboding enveloped her. She'd have to have a talk with her brother about manners—a good hard talk the moment he came back. But oh, how she dreaded it. Lately her talks had met with considerable deafness on his part—or anger.

She sat back down with the others. Elizabeth leaned toward her. "How is the teaching going?"

"Well, I think. The most difficult part is getting some of the local children to show up regularly. Last Tuesday I caught several boys heading toward Old Town to watch the horse races."

"Perhaps you won't have long to worry about such things," said Emma. "You will settle down with some lucky man and start your own family. Except, of course, that would mean the town would need to hire another teacher." She laughed softly.

Rachel tensed at her words. Although none of these folks knew much about her past, she'd already spent most of her life taking care of her father and Caleb, following the whim of a man caught up in gold fever. She forced a smile and tried to keep her voice light. "Oh, I don't know. I rather like making my own way at the moment."

Terrance raised his brows. "I should think marriage, taking care of one man and raising his children would be enough to satisfy a woman."

A slow burn started inside her. "I like teaching. And I'm good at it. Don't I have a responsibility to use this gift?"

"Yes," Terrance said, frowning slightly. "Of course, for your own children."

"Ah-hem." Reverend Crouse placed his napkin carefully by his plate, signaling that supper—and this conversation—was over. She bit back her retort. "Rachel, if you're still set on riding out to the lighthouse, we'll go first thing in the morning."

Terrance paused in taking his last bite of strawberry dessert, looking from the reverend to Rachel. "Uh…if you don't mind my asking, what business do you have at the lighthouse?"

"I want to invite Mr. Taylor and his daughter to attend services," the reverend answered.

Terrance quickly covered his mouth with his napkin, subduing a snort. "Good luck, then. He's been living out there for nearly a year and this week was only the third time I've ever seen him in the store. He's a lost cause—his daughter, too. You shouldn't waste your time on those two."

"Lost causes are the Lord's specialty," the reverend said, rising to his feet. "And I'm beginning to believe Rachel's too."

The others followed suit. Amid compliments to Rachel and Emma for the fine dinner, they gravitated toward the parlor to play games.

Terrance stayed behind as Rachel began to clear the table. "Excellent meal, Rachel."

"Thank you." It had better be edible; she had been cooking since she was fourteen. "Oh, you don't need to help—"

A loud knocking on the front door interrupted her.

"Rachel?" Reverend Crouse called. "You'd best come here."

She put down the dirty plates and walked into the parlor. Sheriff Thorne stood in the entryway holding firm to Caleb.

"Miss," he acknowledged her and then the small group, sweeping his battered hat off belatedly. "Perhaps we'd better take this out on the porch so your guests can carry on."

She nodded and followed him outside, feeling Terrance's presence behind her. Thorne was the town's part-time sheriff, splitting his time between La Playa and Old Town San Diego. She didn't know him well, but he drew a lot of respect from the people here. "What is going on?"

"I caught your brother with his friends, startin' a fire

down by the old hide houses. A fire this time of year could destroy the whole town."

Her brother hung his head and didn't look at her.

"This is one more mishap in a line of minor scrapes, miss. You're his guardian. I'd suggest you keep a closer eye on him."

She nodded, acknowledging the responsibility. She couldn't believe Caleb would try something so foolish on his own. It had to be the coercion of the other two boys. "Have you got anything to say?" she asked her brother.

His jaw set, he glared at her from under his red brows and shook his head.

"Then go to your room. We'll talk about this later." He shuffled past her and inside the house.

She turned back to the sheriff. "Thank you. I'll watch him more closely." She didn't know how she could, but she'd try. Every day Caleb pulled further and further away from her. She was losing him. Her one bit of family left.

Sheriff Thorne touched his hat. "Sorry to intrude upon your day."

She watched him stride down the steps and back toward the Custom House that held the small, makeshift jail.

Terrance stepped onto the porch from the doorway. "I'll help the best I can, Rachel. Boys can be tough."

A heavy sigh escaped. "He won't listen to me anymore. Not like when he was younger."

"His father should be the one looking out for him," Terrance said. "Not you."

Rachel pressed her lips together. Her father hadn't

taken much of an interest in either of them since her mother passed away. He'd just been interested in finding gold. If only Caleb had someone who could help him through this rocky stage. She certainly wasn't much help. The tighter she held on, the harder he pulled away. Plus she worried about how Caleb's actions would affect her standing in the community. The selfish thought nudged her and she felt small for thinking it. But she still worried. Teaching was her livelihood—and Caleb's too, for the time being.

Terrance cleared his throat. "About tomorrow. I… wish you would reconsider about going out to the lighthouse. It will be a long ride, and Taylor won't take you up on your offer."

"I don't shirk a challenge, Mr. Morley. The girl needs to be in school and I'm going to convince him of it."

By the look on his face, it wasn't the answer he'd wanted. "Nothing I say will dissuade you?"

"My mind is made up." She didn't add that the more students she had in school, the better job security for her, although the thought had crossed her mind a time or two since seeing the girl.

"It seems like everyone dislikes him. Are they true— the things I've heard?" But even she could hear the beginning of doubt in her voice.

"Rumors have some truth to them in most cases. Otherwise how would they start?"

She shook off the misgivings. "I'm sure I'll be safe enough with Reverend Crouse."

"Yes…well," he said, his gaze hardening slightly,

"you know how I feel about you going out there. It's a fool's errand."

He waited. Probably still hoping she'd change her mind. When she didn't say more he continued. "Thank you for supper. Until Sunday services then."

She nodded and watched him walk down the porch steps to the street. Sunday was the furthest thing from her mind.

Chapter Three

Reverend Crouse yanked sharply on Jericho's reins to avoid a large dried rut in the dirt road, yet their carriage still bumped through the edge, jostling Rachel to one side. She grabbed her seat and smiled gamely. "I hope after all this, we find them at home."

"I don't know where else they would be. Light keepers as a rule must not leave their lamps unattended."

"Well, that gives us a place to start, then," she said, thinking of her brother and how easily he slipped out of sight whenever he wanted to. "Trying to tie Caleb down and keep track of him is not easy."

Reverend Crouse chuckled. "It may seem that way now, but you're doing the right thing. Caleb will be the better for it in the long run. He's not a bad boy, he just needs direction."

"I suppose." Rachel sighed, thinking her brother more and more showed signs of being like his father. "I'm glad you had chores for him to do today."

"Terrance Morley stopped by earlier. He has things Caleb can help with at the mercantile."

She shook her head. "Caleb needs something physical. He's never been one for being cooped up inside. Often he talks about joining up with the whalers. And I'm afraid he might. That would suit him."

The reverend skirted another deep rut where rainwater had gouged out the quickest path to the sea several hundred feet below. To Rachel's left glistened the deep-blue waters of the harbor, and to her right the ocean stretched out unbroken to the horizon. Stunted light-green sagebrush and chaparral lined both sides of the road, struggling to keep a foothold in the dry ground. No homesteads broke the monotony of the single dirt road they traveled, a road that striped the ridge of the peninsula like the line down a lizard's back.

Jericho pulled the carriage up one last rise and the lighthouse came into view. The sandstone house and tower stood sharply defined against the brilliant blue of the Pacific sky. Two short chimneys straddled the peak at each end of the two-story roof, the far one emitting small burps of black smoke. The light tower rose straight up through the center of the roof's peak. She searched the black iron catwalk that circled the lamp for any sign of the inhabitants.

The reverend stopped Jericho at the picket fence that surrounded the lighthouse and enclosed a small, barren yard and the shriveled remains of a garden. "He's home, all right," he murmured, his eyes focused on the opening door.

Mr. Taylor stepped outside, his shoulders dwarfing

the size of the doorway, his mouth set in a tight scowl as he slipped his shoulder suspenders into place. He wore a cream-colored muslin shirt, open at the collar on this warm and windy day, and dark brown pants that, as his clothes yesterday, appeared serviceable.

A small thrill went through her. What was it about this man that his very presence commanded attention? Would he lump her with all the other people from town? Most likely. She sat straighter in her seat, the urge to prove him wrong infusing her with courage. She wasn't here for him, but she did need his support regarding his daughter.

"Hello. Mr. Taylor, is it?" Reverend Crouse climbed from the carriage. "I'm Reverend Crouse and this is Rachel Houston, the schoolteacher in town. We've come to invite you and your child to Sunday services."

If it were possible, the light keeper's scowl deepened further. His gaze flicked to Rachel, still seated in the carriage, and then settled back on the reverend. "Then you've wasted your trip, Pastor. I'm not on speaking terms with God."

The blunt reply surprised Rachel, but the reverend seemed unruffled. "If not for yourself," the reverend continued, "surely you want your daughter growing in the faith."

Sarcasm twisted Mr. Taylor's mouth. "I'm certain the good people of La Playa want nothing to do with her or me. You must have heard about what happened at the mercantile." This time his stormy gaze settled on Rachel.

She swallowed hard, unable to look away, and felt her heartbeat quicken.

"An unfortunate incident, to be sure," said the reverend as he swept off his black-brimmed hat. "You'll find Hannah is treated better in church."

Taylor turned back to Reverend Crouse, and Rachel took the moment to descend from the carriage and approach the two men. "That has not been my past experience."

Reverend Crouse's silver brows knitted together. "We are not a group of perfect people. Everyone is welcome in God's house."

Mr. Taylor didn't answer, but his eyes hardened to blue slate. He folded his arms across his chest. "Look, Pastor, I mean no offense, but it's best if you just leave. It's too bad you had to ride all the way out here just to hear me say no, but no it is."

The reverend shrugged his shoulders and gave a brief smile. "There is always that chance in my line of work. However, my job is to sow the seeds. Only God can make them grow."

He seemed on the verge of continuing in the same vein, but then pulled back. "Very well. I won't press you further. Remember, though, the invitation stands in the event you change your mind."

"Good day, Pastor."

"One more thing," the reverend continued, smoothly filling in the awkward quiet. "We are planning to hold the annual community picnic here in a few weeks. You weren't here last year, so I wanted to forewarn you."

Taylor pressed his lips together. "Thanks for the warning."

Concern softened Reverend Crouse's eyes. "You're welcome to attend, of course."

Mr. Taylor nodded his acknowledgment.

"Come, Rachel." The reverend started back to the carriage along the hard dirt path.

When she didn't move, Mr. Taylor's steely gaze fastened on her. She swallowed hard. He made it difficult to breathe, let alone speak. It seemed he really hated their intrusion into his life. "I…I brought something for Hannah."

Conscious of being watched, she walked to the carriage boot, and withdrew her present. She'd wrapped it in a large scrap of brown cloth to protect it from the dust on the trip. Perhaps Mr. Taylor would be angry about the gift. Perhaps it would remind him about the incident in the mercantile and he'd refuse it. She hadn't thought of that when wrapping it, and now that made her nervous. But when she turned back to him, she caught a glimpse of his daughter peeking around the door frame. Curiosity and shyness warred on the young girl's face, and Rachel's confidence grew. This wasn't about Mr. Taylor. It was about the girl.

Returning to stand in front of him, she unwrapped the cloth to reveal a papier-mâché doll. Pupilless glass eyes stared up at the light keeper from under painted brown hair. The doll was not new—spidery, hairline cracks ran along the chest and shoulders—but Rachel hoped Mr. Taylor would let Hannah have it. She drew back the cloth further to reveal the green satin gown that had dressed the doll at the mercantile. "The dress fit perfectly. I thought Hannah might give my doll a good home."

Mr. Taylor's brows drew together. "We don't want your charity."

"That's good, because I'm the least charitable person I know," she said, her anger surfacing. "You've already paid for the dress. Sarah sits in a box under my bed day in and day out. She needs a little girl to play with again."

"I'm sure there are plenty of girls at your school. What about them?"

Frustration knotted within her. "I want Hannah to have Sarah."

He continued to watch her silently.

She was not going to back down!

"Do you bribe all children this way?"

He would think such a thing! She struggled to keep her voice low so that Hannah would not hear her anger. "You, sir, are being ridiculously suspicious of a simple kindness. This is not a bribe. And I do not appreciate your rudeness over a simple gift!"

"Perhaps I've had a little experience with Greeks bearing gifts," he said. But he turned to stare at his daughter in the open doorway. Hannah's heart-shaped face was filled with anxious hope. Tangles of blond hair fell over her thin shoulders and onto the same brown dress she'd worn at the mercantile. Timidly, Hannah inched down the stone walk to stand behind her father.

Rachel glanced up at Mr. Taylor but his closed expression told her nothing. A shiver stole through her as she watched him. He was a formidable man, standing a full head taller than her, and she was not a small woman. Yet, he hadn't actually refused the gift. She squatted to the child's level and then held out the doll. "This is Sarah. She was my doll when I was little. I brought her for you."

Hannah glanced up at her father and then slowly reached for the doll, her eyes filled with wonder. She pressed Sarah against her in a hug.

Rachel smiled and let out the breath she'd been holding.

She rose and met his gaze, determined to ignore his surliness. "I know you said church is out of the question. Would you consider school? Hannah is old enough to be in the first or second grade by now."

His look of incredulity gave her his answer even before he spoke. "Absolutely not."

"Mr. Taylor, you can't keep her isolated out here. She'll never learn that there are decent people in this world. She'll always expect the worst."

Anger flashed in his eyes. "Hannah. Go back inside." He held up a hand, forbidding Rachel to speak again until Hannah had done as she was told. When his daughter was at a distance that she could not hear him, he turned to Rachel. "You were there. You saw how they treated her! They talked as though she couldn't hear."

Rachel remembered all too well the lack of empathy in the mercantile. She was still upset at her friend, Amanda. "It bothered me, too," she admitted. "They just need to get to know her. If you were to bring her to school, I would take extra care with her. You must know that this constant isolation is not good for her."

Her words hung suspended in the air between them.

His eyes narrowed, but he seemed to consider her suggestion for the space of an instant. "Prove it. You tutor her."

Startled, she met his gaze. "Tutor her? But that's not what I meant!"

He waited, watching her closely.

The thought took hold. Could she do it? She had so little teaching experience, and Hannah was not an ordinary student. Did she have what it would take to help her? She swallowed hard, intrigued with the idea.

She met his gaze. Was that hope in his eyes beneath the hardness? Perhaps he was reaching out. In his own way, he was asking for help and she suspected he was a man who seldom asked for anything. He confused her—and he fascinated her.

But how could she agree to his offer? If the school board got wind of any arrangement, she'd lose her job for sure. They wouldn't see it as her teaching Hannah. They'd see it as an unmarried woman visiting an unmarried man—without an escort. It could jeopardize her employment at the school.

"I…I'm sorry, but I haven't the time," she said, her excuse sounding weak, even to her ears. "As I said, bring her to school. I'll see she's looked after and not hurt by the others."

He shook his head. "Why should I trust you any more than the others?"

"I guess you have no reason to. It's just tha—"

"Just forget I asked. I'll teach Hannah what she needs to know."

"You must understand, Mr. Taylor—"

He shut her out. "The reverend is waiting. You better leave now."

She felt her chance slipping away. "Mr. Taylor. I really do want what's best for Hannah."

"You've made your point, Miss Houston. Apparently, we're at a standoff. I won't change my mind." He walked past her and then headed to the carriage where Reverend Crouse waited.

Well that didn't go as planned, she thought. Disheartened, she followed him and let him help her up onto the burgundy-cushioned seat. Her fingers tingled where he steadied her with his callused hand. Unsettled, she busied herself adjusting her skirt about her knees even as she felt him continuing to study her. Then her curiosity got the better of her. "The other day at the mercantile…"

He nodded curtly, listening though she sensed he was impatient for her to leave.

"What did you mean when you said I should believe everything I hear?"

"Why don't you ask that friend of yours? She seemed to know it all."

"I prefer to know the truth."

He just stared at her.

She refused to be baited—handsome or not—and plunged on. "Amanda said you killed your wife."

Beside her, Reverend Crouse inhaled sharply and grabbed the reins. "Rachel! That's quite enough. I believe we have just overstayed our welcome."

Stubbornly she notched up her chin. "If one can call this a welcome at all." She wasn't about to back down. Mr. Taylor had dared her. "She said you escaped from prison."

The light keeper leveled his gaze at her and she felt a twinge of remorse.

"Isn't there something in the Bible about gossip, Reverend?" he asked. Suddenly, with the flat of his hand, he struck Jericho's rump. The horse bolted.

"Oh!" Rachel grabbed her hat with one hand and the edge of her seat with the other, holding on tight as the carriage careened away from the yard.

Reverend Crouse struggled with the reins for control and finally maneuvered Jericho into a jerky canter down the dirt road. They neared the rise and Rachel glanced back, fervently hoping Mr. Taylor's palm stung like the bite of a ruler against bare skin. To her keen disappointment, he snapped an obviously fine-feeling hand to his brow in a mocking salute.

Chapter Four

Stuart descended the circular stairway after checking the lamp. It should be good until dawn when he would extinguish it. He sat at the parlor table. Through the window in front of him, he could see the beam from the light above sweep across the peninsula and then out across the moon-dappled water. The strong smell of ocean and sage permeated the room. Opening his logbook, he wrote:

September 16, 1873
11:45 p.m. Mild wind from the northwest. Clear night.
Visitors—Reverend Crouse. Rachel Houston.

He straightened in his chair, stretching his back as he considered how much he should write about the visit. *Invitation to church?* No. It was no one's business but his own. And the less he mentioned about Hannah, the better.

He swiped his hand across his face. Lord, he was

tired. Hannah had been moody and difficult about everything until Miss Houston had come and given her that doll. Then she had disappeared into her room to play.

Miss Houston. Now there was an interesting woman. Outspoken to be sure, but then, words meant only so much. Actions told a lot more about the character of a person—man or woman. And she had character to spare. She sure didn't back down. First, at the mercantile when she stood up to Terrance and then today, when he was her problem.

His head started to nod and he jerked. What the heck were people saying about him in town? He wanted to keep a quiet existence here, not have people talking about him. He'd had little experience with such things before moving here, finding it easier to hide out in more populated areas. He was getting a fast introduction to small-town nosiness.

His head nodded. The pen fell from his hand. He lowered his head to the desk and closed his eyes. *Just for a minute....*

Stuart pushed open the heavy oak door to the captain's cabin. A soft light from the whale-oil lantern illuminated the nooks and crannies of the small room, spilling a rich golden hue on the wooden beams overhead. Linnea sat at the end of his bunk and leaned over a makeshift bed, singing in a low chant to her daughter.

"Linnea?" he whispered.

She placed her finger against her lips. "Hush. She's

nearly asleep." She smiled at him briefly, then continued her song. The dark bruising along her chin had
healed to a yellow color but the shadows beneath her
eyes confirmed his worry that this voyage had not
healed her spirit. She wasn't sleeping. But she hadn't
complained. She never complained anymore.

A thrill rippled through him at the scene in the small
cabin. Three-year-old Hannah lay curled on her side, a
white cotton nightgown covering her chubby limbs and
a matching sleeping bonnet taming her fine blond wisps
of hair. Wet spiked lashes quieted against pale cheeks.
So there had been another battle of wills about bedtime.
He smiled to himself.

Assured that all was well, he returned to the deck.
The last pink rays of sunlight sparkled across the water
as he barked out orders to adjust the sails and take full
account of the northern winds. On the ship's port side
the purple outline of California's southern coast rose
above the sea, the hazy mountains familiar sentinels on
his journey to San Pedro.

Linnea came to his side, pulling her shawl tighter
around her for warmth. The breeze whipped golden
tendrils of her hair across her neck and cheeks.

"She's asleep now."

He nodded his acknowledgment.

"Do you think John's family will come after us?"

"Yes," he said quietly.

"My father, too?"

"Especially your father. We left a mess in San Francisco. They will want to set it right."

"By condemning you."

He kept silent a moment, looking at but not seeing the water. "I killed him. John's family will want revenge, or payment in some way. So will the law."

"Oh, Matthew. I'm sorry to have dragged you into this. I just didn't know where to turn."

Stuart pulled her close, his arm around her shoulder. "You did the right thing. Never doubt that." He felt the rise and fall of her shoulders as she took a deep breath.

"Yet there is one more favor I must ask of you."

He waited.

"Promise me you'll take care of Hannah if anything happens to me."

"Lin—"

"No. I mean it. I've thought about this a lot. We don't know what will happen. John's family and my father have the law on their side. They have all the resources. Our running away looks like we planned John's death. They'll think we are lovers. John accused me of that so many times—I think to rationalize his own lack of fidelity."

"He didn't deserve you."

Her chin trembled. "I should have waited for you, Matthew. I was weak and lonely at that school. I ruined everything."

He squeezed her arm. "We're together now. And don't worry about Hannah. I'll stand by both of you." He looked over the water, subconsciously noting the increase in whitecaps while he tried to figure out what they should do after delivering the cargo to San Pedro. The voyage had given him time, but a reckoning was swiftly catching up.

First Shipmate Saunders approached with a worried

look on his face. "Captain, I don't like the looks o' that horizon." He raised his thick wiry brows toward the stern of the vessel indicating billowing clouds in the distance. A line of dark gray in their belly foretold of the rain within.

"I see it," Stuart said grimly. "If it heads this way we won't be able to use the stars tonight to guide us. We may have a swift race to port. Make sure the crew is prepared."

"Aye, sir." Saunders hesitated.

"What is it?"

"Touhy stands watch tonight."

Stuart considered the level of experience of the younger man. "Have him wake me if the wind changes course."

"Aye, sir. Can't help thinkin' one of Mr. Lansing's steamers would have been a better choice for this trip."

"Only our ten-year friendship makes it possible for you to say that, Saunders," Stuart said with a sternness he knew his first shipmate would see right through. "The *Maiden* is old, but fit. Rather like you," he teased lightly. "And she's mine, not Dorian's. That makes all the difference on this particular voyage."

With a salute—and a wink—Saunders left.

That night Stuart awoke from his makeshift pallet on the floor. He sensed a change, a creaking of the ship as though forced on a new course. In the bed, Linnea slept fitfully, her soft breath puffing against the sheets. He rose and dressed quickly.

Above deck the light breeze of the evening before had transformed into a bitter gale. Stuart searched the

Kelp, seaweed and a plank of wood had tangled about the *Maiden*'s ladder. There was no hope in untangling the floating mass. He would have to cut them loose.

"Hold my legs!" he shouted at Saunders and grabbed the large knife he carried in his belt. He inched forward until more than half his body hung over the bow and then sawed at the thick hemp rope. In short time the rope gave way and they were free. Winded, he inched back into the boat and sprawled on the seat to catch his breath.

A swell rose fifteen feet above the lifeboat like a vengeful Poseidon rising from the deep. Stuart watched in horror as the swell broke at its apex and crashed down on them. The turbulence battered him, pushing saltwater into his eyes and filling his mouth. He gripped anything he could hold on to, climbing over his crew, trying to reach Linnea. When the water calmed enough to see again, surprisingly the boat still floated right side up.

But Linnea and Hannah were gone.

"Cap'n, don't do it!"

He heard Saunders yell, felt hands reach for him, but there was no time to wait.

He dived in.

Groping frantically through the water, he searched for Linnea and Hannah. The waves shoved him about like a plaything. Kelp tangled around his legs, pulling at him, binding him.

Something drifted across his face—seaweed? More kelp? He struggled closer. In vain he tried to see through the murky waters. Then something bumped against him. He reached—and his hands closed on cloth. Hannah! He pulled her close, and suddenly Linnea was there, too, grasping his forearm with both hands.

Renewed strength flowed through him. He kicked hard for the surface, struggling with the weight of the two. His lungs burned with the need for air.

Lightning flashed above him. The surface was so close, so close. His legs muscles tightened into knots. He forced himself to keep kicking, straining. He had to breathe, had to reach the surface. Then Linnea's hold loosened and he felt her hands slide down his arm. He tried to grasp her, but her fingers slipped through his. He reached again—and his hand closed on nothing but water.

Stuart woke with a start, disoriented, his body coated in sweat. He stared at the logbook on the desk, seeing it without knowing where he was, what it meant. He struggled to get his bearings. His heart pounded, yet quiet surrounded him. Through the window flashed a beam from the lamp, the circular pattern somehow familiar and settling. He buried his face in his hands.

The dream had come again.

He drew in a deep breath to steady his heartbeat, then closed the logbook and rose from his seat. It had been months since he'd dreamed of it—almost a year. He longed for the night it would leave him for good, and yet he feared it, too. The dream was his punishment for not protecting the woman he loved. Yet, in the dream he could still feel her touch and hear her voice.

He climbed the stairs to Hannah's room and leaned

against the door frame, studying her. At least he'd never forget Linnea's face. Hannah was her mirror image. She slept on, her new doll crushed beside her.

That doll.

The events of yesterday rushed back into his thoughts. He'd been rude to Reverend Crouse and Miss Houston. But he wouldn't apologize for his blunt words nor would he place his trust in a God who allowed an innocent woman like Linnea to drown. Still, he did feel a twinge of remorse. Hannah surely liked that doll.

Back in his bedroom he poured cool water into his bowl, then splashed it on his face. His hand strayed to the raised quarter-inch-wide slash that started just over his right brow and extended into his hairline. The angry red mark never let him forget it was his fault Linnea had died…his fault Hannah no longer talked or laughed.

Odd, when he thought over the previous day, how the vision of Miss Houston formed in his mind sharper than that of Linnea. She was nothing like Linnea, who had been soft and biddable. Miss Houston seemed all strong angles and had a decidedly sharper tongue. She certainly hadn't been cowed by him—not with that parting question about prison time. Still, her urging to start Hannah in school nagged at him. Linnea would have insisted on private tutors long before now.

He'd said he could teach Hannah himself, but he wasn't sure he could. He knew all about shipping, about commanding a schooner or steamer and bartering the best price for goods. That wouldn't do Hannah any good. Was he selfish in wanting her to stay here with him? She needed to learn of life beyond the peninsula—

but at what cost? All he wanted to do was protect her. His gut twisted. He'd done a damn poor job of that so far.

He could throttle Miss Houston for stirring up the ashes, for bringing back the nightmare. And that doll! He knew better than to accept it. Why had he? Now his conscience would prick him every time Hannah played with it—and he would think of *her*.

Chapter Five

San Francisco

Dorian Lansing hurriedly mounted the steps of his mansion on Nob Hill, his walking cane tapping a rapid-fire cadence across the smooth-tiled entrance.

"Rose! Rose! Confound it, Whitlow, take these." He shoved his cloak and top hat at the butler. "Where is that woman!"

"In the dayroom, sir…. Dr. Garrett is with her."

Dorian dropped his cane in the wrought-iron rack by the door and headed down the hall. His wife lounged with her feet on the couch, still dressed in her pearl-colored morning robe. At least she'd allowed Mattie to draw her hair back with a pink ribbon today in deference to the doctor's visit.

Dr. Garrett stood as Dorian entered the room. The heavy drapes remained closed against the light of day. No air stirred.

"You're home early, dear," Rose said in her birdlike voice. He detected a slight trembling of her hands.

"May I have a word with you, Mr. Lansing?" Dr. Garrett subtly nodded his head toward the hall.

"Certainly. I'll be right back, Rose." He followed the doctor to the hallway.

"How is she today, Doctor?"

"Thinner, paler."

He'd thought so, too, but to hear his fears out loud made them so much more real. "What else can we do? We've tried everything."

"This is not so much an illness of the body as it is an illness of the spirit. You must find something that captures her interest. She needs a reason to continue living."

Dorian thanked the man and dismissed him. A reason for living! Of all the nerve. Apparently taking care of her husband and household wasn't enough of a reason! Disgruntled, he strode into the dayroom, crossed the parquet floor to a southern window and drew back the heavy burgundy drapes.

"Please…leave that closed." Rose struggled to sit taller. "What did the doctor say?"

He left the drapes as they were and began plumping the pillows at her back, avoiding her gaze. "Nothing new. You're doing just fine."

She caught his hand and motioned for him to sit. She didn't ask why he was early today. He knew better than to hope for a show of interest from her. It had been years since he'd seen any spark in her eyes. He dragged a straight-back chair near and sat. This was his last hope.

"I have information regarding Linnea."

The muscles in her neck worked convulsively as she swallowed. After Rose's panic attack a year ago, the doctor had said not to bring up the accident or the past, but to wait for her to mention it first. So far, she never had.

By God, he'd had enough. Enough! He was not the type to sit around and take this situation a moment longer. He was through with waiting. "I heard from Miss Forester's School for Young Ladies. The headmistress there confirmed my suspicions. She knew John Newcomb well."

"That means…"

The plaintive plea in her voice knifed through him, and he turned from her, unable to bear seeing her hurt more. "Yes. John married our daughter to get his hands on her inheritance. He used her just as we suspected." Dorian kept quiet about the mistress. Such information was not for a genteel lady's ears.

"Oh, Dory."

The reproachful tone set him off. "She should have known better!" His voice quaked with anger. "How could she have been so gullible as to let a man like that into her life? She was a Lansing, for God's sake. Why didn't she listen to me?"

Rose dropped her gaze and turned from him.

"I know what you're going to say, Rose. But I was angry. And frustrated."

"And you turned her away when she finally did come to us for help," she said dully.

"She had to learn to live with her choices. Make the best of it." He took his wife's frail hand. "Well, no matter now. She is gone and we cannot change the past.

But for certain, the child, our granddaughter, belongs with us."

"Matthew is still involved, isn't he? That's why he hasn't come back."

Dorian stiffened at hearing that name and chose to ignore her question. He'd kept the part about the murder from his wife. She'd suffered enough. But he knew Matthew was involved, whether the rumors of adultery were true or not, it was his gun found on the docks. He'd probably pulled the trigger. "I've decided to hire another detective. Randolph has given me a name."

A flash of fear crossed Rose's face.

"I know we had little luck with the first one. I'm willing to try again. More important, are you?"

Her shaking grew worse, but when she looked up at him, her gaze was resolute. "Yes. Do try. It's time we were a family again." She drew a breath and added, "Even...even Matthew."

Dorian felt a sickening lurch in his gut and hardened his heart at her words. "I don't want to hear that man's name spoken in this house or have you forgotten that?"

Rose visibly shrank in front of him. "No. I've not forgotten. But Linnea ran to Matthew. And he took her in. He loved her—as a brother would and...and possibly more."

"Confound it!" He beat his fist on the arm of the couch. "The girl belongs with us. He isn't her father." The hate boiled up inside, choking him.

"But the things you said—"

"He as good as killed Linnea. Matthew murdered our daughter."

Rose shrank away from him and lay back against her cushions. "Oh, Dory. Do what you must. I want nothing more than to find Hannah. She belongs here. This is her birthright. Bring her home any way you can."

Dorian took her hands in his. "If there is a way on earth to find her, I will. And when I do, Matthew will have no choice but to hand her over to me." The vengeance in his voice surprised even him. Slowly he loosened his grip. "I'll take care of everything."

Chapter Six

The strong September sun had finally burned away the fog that hovered each morning over the peninsula. Rachel lifted her face to its warmth for a moment and then glanced behind her. Two wagons and five carriages loaded with churchgoers and food snaked their way to the point like an army of determined ants.

She sat in the bed of the wagon, one arm resting on a picnic hamper, the other holding tight to the wooden side. She had spent all of yesterday baking. Her mouth watered at the thought of the pies nestled between the slow-baked beans and cold chicken.

"So, how much longer do I have to put up with this prison sentence?" Caleb asked from his sprawled position beside her. "Haven't I been okay for the past couple weeks?"

"The sheriff said at least two months," Rachel answered. "You're lucky he didn't put you in jail for starting that fire."

Caleb scowled. "No one cares about those hide houses anyway. One less wouldn't hurt anything."

"But they aren't your property!" she said, exasperated with his attitude. "Besides, you could have torched the entire town. It was irresponsible."

He clamped his hands over his ears to shut out her voice and glared at her. After a few minutes he looked up at Reverend Crouse. "Is the light keeper coming to our picnic, Reverend?"

Rachel tensed. It had been three weeks since her visit with Mr. Taylor and three weeks spent pondering the man. Impulsively, she'd even ordered a book on sign language from back east, just in case it could help the young girl.

"He's welcome, as is anyone," Reverend Crouse answered her brother. "After all, this is a *community* picnic."

"It's not a good idea," Caleb said.

Reverend Crouse glanced over his shoulder. "Why do you say that?"

"'Cause he shot at those fisherman a while back. He's not right in the head. Living out here has made him crazy. Enrique said—" Caleb stopped at the amused look in Reverend Crouse's eyes.

"Don't believe everything you hear. Rumors have a way of growing and changing over time."

"I still say you shoulda had the picnic somewhere else."

They crested the last brush-covered rise and saw the lighthouse. When they neared, Mr. Taylor stepped through the open front door, his jaw set tight. Resentment radiated from him, thick and strong.

"Look at him." Heaviness lodged in the pit of Rachel's stomach. "He doesn't want us here."

"Whether he does or not is of no concern. This is government property. The town has had a picnic here for the past seven years." He stopped Jericho at the gate. "In any case, I'll ask if he and his daughter would like to join us."

Rachel couldn't hear what was said between Reverend Crouse and Mr. Taylor but watched while Hannah inched up to her father and tucked her hand in his. She looked once in Rachel's direction. A moment later she slipped back into the darkness of the house. Mr. Taylor soon followed his daughter and firmly shut the door.

The reverend climbed back into the wagon. "We're welcome to enjoy the view but he prefers not to join us." He clucked at Jericho, urging the horse on, and then waved at the others to follow.

"What of Hannah? She might like the games later," Rachel asked.

"He'll keep the girl with him."

Rachel didn't understand the ambivalence she felt. She'd worn her favorite navy-blue skirt and white blouse, trying to appear tailored like the perfect teacher in order to impress them. And she'd packed enough food in the hope that Hannah and even Mr. Taylor would join them. But now, learning they wouldn't, a wave of relief washed over her. Perhaps she could relax now and simply enjoy the day.

A hundred feet farther, Reverend Crouse pulled the wagon to a stop on a stretch of level ground. Rachel spread out their large quilt with the faded star design between two small sagebrushes. The wind swirled and caught the edges of the makeshift tablecloth whipping it about. "Caleb! Help me, please!"

Amanda Furst caught a corner as Caleb caught the other.

"Didn't want you sailing off," Amanda said.

Rachel glanced up from anchoring her corner with a rock. Amanda, as always, looked prim and proper in her brown satin dress. "Why, thank you."

Amanda nodded toward the lighthouse. "He won't join us?"

"Mr. Taylor was invited, along with his daughter," Rachel answered. "He said no."

"Well, at least he has some common sense." Amanda stood and twirled her parasol over one shoulder. "He would make us all uncomfortable. He treated me abominably in the mercantile."

"He was just looking out for his daughter. And we *were* gossiping."

Amanda raised her chin. "I don't gossip. I was telling the truth."

Why Rachel should feel the least bit protective of Mr. Taylor, she couldn't fathom, but she thought a change in topic was warranted to keep the peace. "I see your brother is here," she said, nodding toward where a few men were setting up tables.

Amanda wrinkled her nose. "Trying to get on Mother's good side. He's up to something."

"I hope he stays clear of my brother." Sam was well-known as the town terror. A few years older than Caleb, he had harassed her brother more than once when she and Caleb had first arrived at La Playa.

Amanda nodded. "Me, too. I suppose Mr. Morley will be sitting with you?"

Rachel stopped pulling things from the basket and looked up. "I'm not sure. He has relatives visiting from San Diego. I imagine they're talking business."

"Oh." Amanda blushed. "Well…that's nice. I, ah, better get back to help Mother." She spun around and returned to where her family was setting out food.

Rachel sat back on her heels. Amanda was interested in Terrance! Before the thought registered any further, a flash of white from the lighthouse drew her eye.

Hannah stood on the catwalk, her chin on the railing, watching the people below. Rachel started to wave a greeting, but then lowered her hand when Mr. Taylor appeared behind the girl and placed his hands on her shoulders. Without turning, Hannah reached up and grasped one of his hands. Such a small gesture, full of trust and innocence. And with it Rachel's heart softened considerably toward the light keeper.

As if he felt her watching, Mr. Taylor's gaze caught hers…and held. Something tenuous reached out to her. Almost without realizing it, she rose to her feet, her gaze still locked on his. The wind picked up the ribbons on her bonnet and tickled her cheek, but she barely noticed. His eyes held hers as though he tried to read her thoughts, see into her soul. Before she could muddle through the strange sensation, he pulled Hannah back from the walkway and disappeared from sight.

Rachel let out the breath she had been holding and turned back to setting out the tin plates and napkins. Her cheeks flamed with heat as she tried to concentrate on the dishes, but could only see his face before her. Even her breasts tingled with awareness of him.

Caleb lugged over another basket and dumped it awkwardly in the middle of the quilt.

"My pies!" She reached out and righted the hamper, glad to have a diversion from her thoughts of the light keeper. She held up a squashed cherry pie in her hand. "To think it made the trip all the way here, and then to end up as flat as a sand dollar."

"Where's the problem, Rach? I'll eat it, anyway."

She lowered the pie, placing a cloth napkin beneath to protect the faded quilt. "No matter, I guess," she said grudgingly. "It will still taste the same. Besides, we have the apple pie, and there will be ice cream later. Just try to be more careful." Caleb was getting clumsier every week. Lately he reminded her more of a disjointed rag doll, all elbows and knees, than a flesh-and-blood boy.

Across the quilt from her, Reverend Crouse rose awkwardly, pressing on his knee with one hand. Skirts and coats rustled as those assembled stood for the blessing. Once he was finished, everyone gathered around the tables piled with food to fill their plates.

At Rachel's makeshift table, the chicken pieces disappeared quickly. Rolls with butter and then molasses cookies followed. Caleb sectioned off a large piece of mashed cherry pie and ate it with boyish gusto. Rachel had just put her tin plate back in the basket when Terrance strolled up.

"Hello, Rachel."

He towered over her, pulling on one end of his

drooping mustache. He nodded to the reverend, Emma and Caleb in turn, and then his gaze locked on her to the exclusion of the others. What was it that Amanda found appealing about him?

"Ready for that walk?"

She glanced over at the other picnickers. They were finishing their meals. "What about starting the children's games?"

With a wave of her hand, Emma Crouse intervened. "Oh, go on now, you two. I still remember a game or two. And Caleb can help me."

Terrance pulled Rachel to her feet. "It's settled, then." He offered his arm.

He led her along the perimeter of the peninsula. From this high position, she could see a steamer leaving the harbor. Two ships headed toward San Diego, their white sails taut against the wind as they navigated the deepest part of the channel.

A burst of laughter and giggles came from behind her. Rachel looked back toward the picnickers. Emma and Elizabeth organized the boys and girls for the three-legged races, handing out long strips of cloth to bind legs together.

"I should get back and help," Rachel said, starting to release Terrance's arm. She glanced again at the children and Elizabeth. Where was Caleb?

Terrance patted her hand back into place. "Those children get you all week. They can do without you for a few more minutes."

Reluctantly, she allowed herself to be led toward the ocean side of the point. Here the ground dropped steeply down hundreds of feet. Sagebrush and scruffy vegetation covered the higher ground, but in two areas, the wind had bitten into the high land, carving naked sandstone cliffs. Far below, the waves beat against their base. "Is that a beach down there?"

"A small one. You can't see much from here."

She searched for something to say. "How are your cousins from San Diego enjoying their stay?" she asked.

"They're hoping to see a whale or two while here. So far there haven't been any."

"I'm not sure it's the season for them," she said, trying to remember what a Portuguese whaler had recently told her in town.

Terrance stopped walking and faced her. "Rachel, ah, I don't quite know how to say this."

She glanced up at him. "Just say what's on your mind. I don't bite."

He offered a weak smile. "You know that I sit on the school board."

"Yes."

"Well, the others have asked me to inquire into your qualifications."

Suddenly concerned, she met his gaze. "But they've already done that—when they interviewed me. They don't think I'm doing a good job?"

"No, it's not that."

He ran a hand through his straight hair, and she noticed a pink tinge to his usually pale face.

"Will you be taking the teacher examination this year?"

"I plan to—after studying more. Probably in early spring."

"Oh…well, then. That should appease them," he said, but he wasn't looking her in the eye.

She tried to remain calm, but her insides were in turmoil. She needed this work. "Would they hire someone else? Someone with a certificate in place of me?"

He hesitated in answering at first. "I'll be honest."

"I would prefer it," she said, her alarm growing.

"A few of the board are talking about it."

"Terrance, they hired me knowing I didn't have that piece of paper. And I promised to work toward it. Surely they can give me a little more time. At my interview they said they understood my experience in Wisconsin was as valuable as that certificate."

He stepped close, and this time he did meet her eyes. "I'll talk to them. I, for one, want to keep you happy. If that means teaching for a year or two, so be it."

"Thank you." Her smile trembled a little. "You know my schooling has been haphazard. There are gaps in it because my father moved us around so much. But I'll study and be ready for the test in the spring. You can count on me."

"I know. And I'm sorry to worry you."

"I need this job, Terrance. Caleb and I—we both do."

He nodded his acknowledgment just as a chorus of lively shouts rose behind them. "Maybe we should join in the games now."

She smiled slightly. After all, this was a picnic and she intended to have a good time. "Let's join in the race. I promise I won't trip you."

He raised a brow. "Think we'll make a good team?"

"Of course," she said quickly, then realized as he continued to watch her that he wasn't talking about the race at all. She swallowed hard. Did her job depend on her relationship with Terrance?

They neared the lighthouse, and she glanced once more at the empty catwalk. She had to talk with Mr. Taylor before she left today. Just once more—to encourage him to send Hannah to school. It was best for the girl, and it wouldn't hurt her own job security to have another steady student.

Suddenly a series of loud pops exploded through the air. Someone cried out, and people began running to the cliff's edge. A woman screamed.

Rachel scanned the cluster of people for Caleb. She found him crouched at the edge beside Sam Furst. Her heart pounded in her chest as she picked up her skirt and raced toward them. What had happened?

Murmurs rose from the group. "It's little Benjamin! Somebody get a rope."

Several men rushed past her, heading for their wagons.

The crowd moved back to allow Reverend Crouse in. Rachel peered over the edge, and then covered her mouth to stifle her cry.

Thirty feet below, seven-year-old Benjamin Alter clung to a small outcropping of sandstone and brush, his stomach flush against the side of the cliff. Blood trickled from a large scrape across his forehead. Hundreds of feet below him, the ground fell away to the foaming ocean and jagged rocks. The boy looked up at them with terrified eyes.

"Hang on, now," Reverend Crouse said. "We're getting a rope."

Rachel's heart pounded in her chest. Ben could lose his grip on the ledge at any minute. She met the reverend's worried gaze. "Surely Mr. Taylor has rope."

Before the words were out of her mouth, the light keeper appeared at her side, a thick coil of rope slung over his shoulder, his manner so commanding that everyone backed away to give him room.

"Help! I can't hold on!" Benjamin yelled.

Caleb grabbed the rope from Mr. Taylor's hands and began tying it around his waist.

Rachel gasped. "Caleb! No!"

"It's my fault he fell," her brother mumbled. "It's my place to get him."

Stuart watched as the boy fumbled with the thick rope at his waist. It was a poor attempt at a knot and one he knew from experience would prove unsafe. Stuart could handle the rope and the climb. He'd climbed among the rigging of schooners being tossed and pitched about by the sea for years. He snapped the rope from the boy's hand. "Step back."

Tying an efficient knot at his own waist, he looked directly at Miss Houston. "Keep Hannah from the edge."

At her wide-eyed nod, he handed the other end of the rope to Terrance Morley, wondering for a moment if he could trust him. But then another man, and then another gripped the rope, their faces set with determination.

Stuart lay down on his abdomen and lowered himself over the cliff's edge. His last look at the handful of onlookers centered on one person—Rachel. Her eyes had clouded with worry. Likely for the boy; surely not for him.

"Don't look up," he yelled down to the boy below. "The loose sand will get into your eyes. And don't move. Let me take hold of you."

Pebbles and loose dirt shot out from beneath his boots as he scrambled down the steep wall of sandstone. All at once his feet met air rather than the cliff and he swung around, smashing his shoulder against the gritty wall. Finally he slid even with the boy.

"Just a minute more and I'll have you. Don't let go yet."

The boy gasped as he struggled to hold on while Stuart wrapped the extra length of rope tightly around the boy's waist and tied a lighterman's hitch. To his credit, the boy remained still as instructed rather than panicking and grabbing hold of Stuart too soon.

"What's your name?" Stuart asked gently.

"B-Benjamin."

The boy couldn't be much older than Hannah.

"Onto my shoulders now," Stuart commanded. "Slide over to my back."

"I can't."

His plaintive voice tugged at Stuart's heart. "Sure you can."

"I'm scared."

"The rope will hold you."

"My hands—they're s-stuck."

Stuart glanced at Benjamin's white-knuckled grip on the ledge and a small tuft of weeds. How had the boy managed to hang on this long?

"Okay. Just do the best you can. I won't let you fall."

Benjamin's eyes filled with unshed tears. Stuart could almost see the boy's mind working, trying to bolster his courage.

"I'll count to three and you grab my neck."

A small nod.

"One…two…three!"

Stuart leaned toward the boy, snaking his arm around Benjamin's waist and hauling him close. He struggled to keep his grip on the rope while the boy locked his legs around Stuart's hips. Frantically, Benjamin grabbed Stuart's shirt then scrambled up and wrapped his arms around Stuart's neck. He could feel the thudding of the boy's heart against his back.

He breathed a sigh of relief. "Good job. You ready now?" He felt Benjamin's nod rub against his back. Looking up, he yelled, "Haul us up!"

The men pulled on the rope, a rhythm building as they heaved against the weight. Stuart braced his feet against the cliff to steady the swinging. Sweat beaded on his forehead. Above, Stuart could see the first man's arm muscles bulging with the effort to draw him up.

Finally he and the boy came flush with the ground at the top of the cliff. Strong hands reached out to grip Benjamin and pull him from Stuart's neck. More men reached down to help Stuart over the edge. He crawled a few feet then sprawled onto his back and gasped for air.

People crowded around congratulating the men who'd held the rope. A few nodded to him by way of thanks, but most seemed a little unsure what to make of him. He rose slowly to his feet.

An elderly couple stopped before him. The old woman dabbed tears from her eyes while she thanked him profusely for saving her grandson.

Stuart nodded once. "Bring him to the house to wash out those scrapes," he said gruffly. Then he began gathering up his rope, ignoring the sting of his rope-burned palms.

"Are you all right?"

Miss Houston's soft Midwestern voice came from behind him, the concern in it catching him off guard. He slung the coil of rope over his shoulder and turned to her. His heart did a quick thud. She surely had fetching green eyes—the kind a man could drown in. And they seemed to hold as much worry as her voice.

"I'm fine."

"Hannah stayed at the lighthouse."

"Good."

She seemed to want to say something more, but Morley and Caleb stepped up. Not anxious to speak with anyone else, Stuart started toward the house. He could feel the eyes of the entire assemblage staring at his back as he walked away.

By the time he'd cleaned himself in the kitchen, someone was rapping on the door. He opened it to Miss Houston and Benjamin, aware his pulse had kicked up a notch again and tried to ignore it. She held out something covered with cloth.

"For you…for helping Benjamin."

"No need." He grabbed a kitchen towel that was

slung over the back of a chair and wiped the water from his neck. "Come in and wash out his scrapes. There's warm water on the stove."

She pursed her lips at his refusal of the gift but still ushered the boy inside. Looking about quickly, she placed the cloth-covered item on the kitchen table. "I wanted to repay you in some way—to thank you. I hope you like apple." She pulled the edge of cloth aside to reveal a pie.

He hesitated, not wanting to take something more from her. First the doll, now this, but it sure looked delicious. With his simple cooking, he and Hannah would never have something so fine. He nodded his acceptance. "Hannah will like it."

She checked the temperature of the water in the pan on the stove, pulled Benjamin's sleeves up to his elbows and slowly submerged his scraped, bloody hands. The boy winced and jerked his hands back at first, but then allowed her to wash them with soap.

She was gentle with the boy, Stuart noticed. Didn't rush him, but let him go at his own pace. He liked that about her. Suddenly he realized she was addressing him.

"Have you given any more thought to bringing Hannah to school? She needs to have a few friends her own age." She wet a nearby washcloth and dabbed at the cut on Benjamin's forehead.

How could she ask again? "Did you see what caused Benjamin to fall, Miss Houston?"

She looked up, surprised. "No. I just heard his scream, and then everybody yelling as they ran toward the cliff. Did you?"

"He was near the edge when two older kids set off the firecrackers right beside him. He jumped at the noise and lost his footing. I don't know if those older boys were being stupid, or whether they were being mean, probably a mixture of both, but I don't want them near Hannah. It's the innocent ones that get hurt. Hannah and I don't want anything to do with those others." He moved closer, breathing in her scent, lowering his voice. "But you can repay me, you know. You tutor Hannah."

She drew a sharp breath, and color rose in her cheeks as she bent to dry Benjamin's cuts with a towel. She was thinking about the proposal all right. He waited—and was perturbed at how much he wanted her to say yes.

She shook her head. "I really can't. It…it wouldn't be proper."

He pulled back. "Hannah's had more hurt in her six years than anyone should have in a lifetime. Propriety be damned."

"Mr. Taylor!" She slid her gaze to Benjamin in warning.

Obviously his cussing hadn't endeared him to her, but it hadn't shocked her, either.

"My coming here wouldn't change anything. She still needs friends, needs school, the socialization. You're not helping her by secluding her out here."

Well, he'd tried. He wouldn't beg. "Thank you for the pie." He started for the circular stairs. "You can see yourself out when you're done."

That night Rachel tossed and turned in bed, pulling the thick covers over her head one moment, then kicking them off the next. Benjamin's narrow escape from death played over and over in her mind. Caleb had said it was his fault Benjamin fell. She could only assume he'd been the one to set off the firecrackers. What was he thinking? And where had Sam run off to? She hadn't seen him again.

Yet, it was the look in Mr. Taylor's eyes just before he had taken the rope from her brother that haunted her. She knew instinctively he would never have let Caleb go over the cliff even though he'd seen him set off the firecrackers. For all the rumors that followed Mr. Taylor, there was something in him quite noble.

When he had opened the door to her, a queer feeling had skittered through her. Water drops splattered his neck and shirt. He'd wet combed his wavy hair and for the first time she could clearly see the jagged scar on his forehead. His clean-shaven face was so different from the bearded, mustached style of most men she knew, but she found his strong chin and the straight line of his nose agreeable—actually more than agreeable.

On the way home, she had spoken to Reverend Crouse about the tutoring. "Absolutely not!" he'd said. "The people of this town wouldn't stand for it. Remember what happened to Martha Carter. The same could happen to you. Besides, Caleb needs a firm hand and where would that leave him?"

The previous teacher, Martha Carter, was seen taking a meal alone with a married man. The school board found out about it and fired her. It had happened more than two years ago, but people still spoke of it. Rachel

He followed as they walked toward the cliff to a place where the ocean spread all the way to the horizon. In the never-ending wind Miss Houston's yellow bonnet ribbons danced across her face and her skirt wrapped around her ankles. He took a second look. She had quite trim ankles.

Caleb inched toward the edge.

Stuart yanked him back. "What in blazes are you trying to do? Tempt fate? I'm not climbing down there again, so stay clear."

Caleb jerked from his grasp and gave him a dark look.

"I mean it," he repeated. "Stay clear of the edge."

The boy's chin jutted out and Stuart again noted the family resemblance with Miss Houston. "Don't treat me like a kid."

Stuart snorted. "Actions say it all."

Caleb eyed him coolly. "I'm just here 'cause my sister is making me come. Says she needs a chaperone. So you watch yourself and keep your hands to yourself."

Stuart stared right back at Caleb. The cocky kid. "She should have a chaperone, especially with Vasquez still running loose in these parts."

The boy's chest deflated an inch at the mention of the Mexican bandit, and then his eyes narrowed. "You, ah, don't happen to know him, do ya?"

Stuart let him worry a good half minute and then shook his head. "No, but it doesn't hurt to be cautious. Your sister shouldn't come here alone. Neither of you should."

"Humph," Caleb mumbled. The prospect of being a chaperone obviously didn't thrill him. After a moment he nodded toward the surf. "Any good fishin' spots down there?"

Stuart pointed farther north. "Off that large flat rock."

"Is there a way down?"

"A trail." After a brief pause he added, "If you live long enough I'll show it to you."

Caleb shrugged his shoulders, the sullen look back on his face.

Suddenly Hannah tugged on Miss Houston's hand and pointed out to sea.

"What is it?" Rachel asked.

Stuart put a hand on Hannah's shoulder and concentrated on the blue-green waters. "I don't see anything." Then he did. Dark shadows moving just beneath the surface. "Porpoises," he breathed.

"Oh! Look! One is jumping!" Miss Houston cried out.

Two more shadows emerged behind the first. Before long another surfaced and jumped.

Her green eyes twinkled. "Caleb, just look at them!"

Her delight pulled at Stuart. He studied her face, entranced. She wore her emotions the way she did her hat. What was it going to be like to have a woman around again? He pushed back the sudden guilt that rose in his chest. A teacher for Hannah was all he wanted. Nothing more. She would be a good influence. Surely Linnea would have agreed with his choice.

Miss Houston knelt by Hannah and pointed out the flat-topped Table Mountain across the border in Mexico. She counted the porpoises when they came up for air, the mist spouting from their blowholes. Strands of dark burnished hair floated free from under her bonnet and mixed with the blond wisps of Hannah's. Both faces were alight with the magic of their find.

In another place, another time, it would have been Linnea beside Hannah. It should have been Linnea now, but for his fumbling rescue attempt. Irritated for allowing himself to remember again, he spun on his heel and headed toward the lighthouse.

It was late. Color had washed from the facades of the town buildings until all looked drab and gray. Rachel urged Jericho down the street toward the parsonage.

Reverend Crouse stood at the back door of the house. He spoke to a short, oriental man with a basket of fish slung over his shoulder. When he saw Rachel and Caleb, he waved the fisherman on, then joined them at the small carriage house. He grabbed Jericho's bridle while Caleb climbed down from the high seat. "Kind of late."

She swallowed hard, feeling Caleb's gaze on her. "Yes. The time got away from me."

Reverend Crouse stared at her for an interminable length of time, during which she clumsily wrapped the reins around the brake lever for storage. "Mind the hour from now on," he said, frowning. "It's getting dark earlier and you shouldn't be out after nightfall."

"I'll be more careful. I'll get supper started."

"Good. Caleb? See to Jericho. Make sure he has plenty of water before you come in."

"Yes, sir." Caleb's shoulders hunched forward, and the mutinous look in his eyes warned Rachel not to get in his way as he rounded the carriage to unhitch the horse. He hadn't wanted to go with her in the first place. She just hoped he'd adjust to her plan and not give it away.

"Rachel—" Reverend Crouse paused. "Mr. Morley is here. He's waiting in the front parlor."

Now what could he want? She didn't need an inquisition from him. Her stomach was in knots as it was.

As she hurried by, the reverend touched her shoulder. "He's a good man," he said gently.

She slanted a look at him.

"Our small congregation thinks highly of the entire Morley family."

She nodded her acknowledgment. "I know you mean well, but I don't care a fig what the rest of the congregation thinks in this matter."

"That'd be your father speaking words right out of your mouth."

"Just because my fath—"

"I know, I know. Your father had his faults just as I have mine. I'm just saying don't be too hasty to dismiss Terrance. I hate to see you all alone in your old age, that's all."

"Caleb is with me."

"That's not the same. Besides, he'll grow up and move on. Then where will you be, Rachel?"

"Right here I hope. After following my father all around the state of California, it seems to me the best thing about Terrance is the fact that he'll probably stay put in one place to run his store."

She ignored the reverend's raised brows and hurried into the house, stopping in the kitchen just long enough to remove her hat and smooth her hair before she walked through to the parlor.

Terrance sat rigidly on the sofa drumming his fingers on the padded arm. She had to admit he looked pleasant enough in his work suit—minus the apron. He jumped to his feet when he saw her. "Hello, Rachel. A package came for you at the store. Thought I'd take the opportunity to deliver it personally." He held out a brown-paper-wrapped box.

She took it and checked the return address. A thrill of excitement started in the pit of her stomach. "Thank you."

"Aren't you going to open it?"

"Not now." She couldn't bear to wait to open the package, but wait she would. It wasn't for Terrance's eyes. "I have to start supper."

"Don't you want to make sure it's what you ordered? I noticed it came all the way from San Francisco."

She was certain what it was. She'd asked Elizabeth to order it more than five weeks ago under strictest confidence. "Later. I'll look at it later."

"Well, I'd better get home then." He paused at the door. "I heard that the light keeper asked you to tutor his daughter."

She swallowed hard. He couldn't know—not in one day, could he? He must have been talking with Reverend Crouse.

He took her hands and held them together, his

fingers as cool as the coins in his store's money box. "I'm surprised the man had the gall to ask you. You are much too busy trying to get the school here off the ground. Did he even consider the cost to your reputation?"

"He's just interested in helping his daughter. I doubt he gave any thought to social etiquette. He's been isolated so long, he probably isn't aware of such things."

Terrance grunted.

"You don't like him much, do you?"

"I don't trust him. Besides, the girl is beyond help."

A burn of indignation started inside her. "She just needs a little guidance."

"Guidance?" His eyes were cynical beneath dark raised brows. "Look, Rachel, you can't go out of your way for someone like her. Mrs. Greensboro or Mrs. Attenberry would do just as well as her teacher. They are both older, widowed."

"And set in their ways. Hannah couldn't relate to them."

In the light of the gas lamp, exasperation showed plainly on his face. "Why are you so interested in this girl? Are you sure your interest doesn't have more to do with Taylor than his daughter?"

Heat raced up her cheeks. "Of course not!" But the words stuck in her throat. The light keeper fascinated her—more than she cared to admit. Even the thought of him had her heart racing faster. But her job was to tutor Hannah, and she wouldn't lose track of that.

Terrance studied her a moment, then glanced once more at the package before stepping outside. "All right.

The school board is meeting tonight and wanted me to find out the date of your teacher's examination."

"In late February. I'll have to travel to Los Angeles."

"I'll let them know. Studying for that will keep you busy. I'll be happy to take you to the stagecoach when the time comes."

She couldn't hold back a small smile. Terrance had unwittingly given her an excuse to be unavailable for the next few months. "I would appreciate that. Thank you."

"Well, I guess this is good night, then."

She closed the door behind him, worried about his dark expression. He couldn't possibly know anything about her visit to the lighthouse today, could he? She couldn't get cold feet—not when she had barely begun.

She flew to her bedroom with the package, shut the door and tore off the brown wrapper. Embossed in black on the front cover were the words: "American Sign Language: From the American Institution for the Deaf and Dumb." She flipped several pages, excitement mounting as she glanced through the book. Hannah could do this!

The back door slammed shut and heavy footsteps sounded in the kitchen. Quickly Rachel shoved the package into a drawer. She squared her shoulders and walked into the kitchen to begin the evening meal.

Chapter Eight

"Hannah! Covering your ears will not help you learn."

They sat in the parlor, Hannah on a stool and Rachel on the tapestry-covered chair near the fire. The coal fire had dwindled to nothing more than an occasional puff of smoke from the hearth. The simple rhymes and ink drawings on the page in front of Hannah had captivated her until Rachel tried to explain the alphabet. Then Hannah slumped in her chair and pressed her hands over her ears.

Rachel sighed. "Perhaps we've done enough for one day. Let's go outside. I should check on Caleb."

On the lighthouse steps, Rachel paused. The wind blew constantly, but over the sound of the wind, she heard a barrage of questions coming from her brother. She found him near the shed with Mr. Taylor. They hunkered over a battered lobster crate, twining wire around and through the slats.

"You ever got your hand caught in one of their

claws?" Caleb asked as he pulled the end of the wire tight. "Did it let go on its own? How'd you get it off?"

Mr. Taylor used pliers to wrap more wire around Caleb's piece and crimp it off. Methodically he tested the strength of the wire and wood around the crate before answering. "I chopped off the claw."

"Oh. Right." Caleb quieted after that.

Rachel stifled a smile and followed Hannah to the lookout bluff. Before turning her attention once more to her teaching, she glanced back at her brother. He had begun his questions again. She cupped her hands to her mouth ready to call to him when Mr. Taylor looked up. At the subtle shake of his head she paused, then lowered her hands.

He certainly was patient with Caleb. She recalled Terrance's irritation whenever her brother had a question. And she'd never seen Terrance without his suit, and with a sheen of sweat on his brow like Mr. Taylor wore now. Reluctantly she turned away and followed Hannah.

Hannah led her to a sandstone hollow, protected from the worst of the wind and warmed by the concentrated afternoon rays of the sun. A footpath in front of them switchbacked down the steep hill until it disappeared far below. Seagulls careened at eye level along the edge of the point floating on the updraft.

Rachel leaned back against the gritty sandstone wall and patted the ground beside her. "I could fall asleep here, it is that comfortable and warm." She fussed with her hair, which the wind had teased from its knot while she mulled over how to broach the subject of signing with Hannah.

"How about drawing a picture for me in the dirt? Anything you like."

Hannah plopped down.

When she ignored her suggestion, Rachel roused herself and picked up a nearby stick. She began drawing a picture. "I used to live far away from here in a place where I could actually smell the earth. Can you even imagine that, Hannah? The dirt was so rich it was nearly black. A person could grow anything they wanted. Here it smells of the sea and sage, and the dirt isn't dirt at all but sand. It is a wonder that anything grows."

She sighed and concentrated on her drawing of a whale. "There, now. I've started it. You finish."

Beside her, Hannah leaned forward, and with her finger fixed the fluke and added a water spout.

"Much better. It did need something more." She leaned back against the wall. "Hannah? How are we going to talk to each other? I want to know what you're thinking—when you understand something, or more often when you don't. Any ideas?"

She watched the parade of thoughts crossing Hannah's face.

"What about talking by using our hands?"

Hannah raised one brow.

Rachel wasn't worried. She had memorized a few choice words, just to get started. "For example, how does this look for a whale?" She held her first three fingers out on her right hand and curved them in front of her left forearm, which she held across her chest. She moved her fingers slowly up and then down. "Can you see the whale going through the waves? You give it a try now. This could be fun. Our own language that no one else knows."

The idea of a secret language worked. Hannah sat up straight and began mimicking Rachel's motions. Rachel did the hand sign for *father,* then *shell,* then *horse.* Hannah copied her movements, repeating them until she got them just right.

After twenty minutes Rachel rose, dusting off the back of her skirt. "That's enough for today. We'll learn more next time."

Stubbornly Hannah crossed her arms over her chest.

It didn't take a teaching certificate to understand this particular look. "Let's go back to the house and I'll give you a few things to work on until my next visit."

Hannah wouldn't budge.

Finally exasperated, Rachel admitted, "I don't know any more words! You should learn the *right* signs—not just made-up ones."

Suspicion entered Hannah's gray eyes.

Rachel sighed. She wanted Hannah to trust her. "It isn't exactly a secret language. Come with me. I'll show you what I mean."

She strode to the carriage boot with Hannah right behind her, grabbed the signing book and placed it in the girl's hands.

"There are others who cannot speak, Hannah. Like you. Children and adults. This is how they talk to each other and their families."

Slowly Hannah flipped through the pages. Slower and slower she studied the drawings. Totally engrossed in the book, she walked to the stone steps of the lighthouse, sat and balanced the book in her lap. Rachel followed quietly.

Behind his daughter, Mr. Taylor appeared in the doorway, wiping his hands on an oily towel. He looked over Hannah's shoulder at the book and his eyes hardened to blue crystal. Reaching down, he pulled the book from her lap and studied the title. His lips pressed together in a grim line. "Hannah. Go inside and set the table for supper," he said in a voice that discouraged any opposition.

Hannah jumped up and ran inside. Rachel suddenly had the uncomfortable thought that her employer might not approve of her methods. He shoved the book at her. "You need to discuss things like this with me first, before wasting Hannah's and your time. She doesn't need this. She'll speak again."

Dismayed, Rachel took the book.

"Understand—I don't want her treated differently. She is no different from any of your other students. Use the methods you use at school. Not this." He strode toward the shed before she could think to reply.

Hannah had made progress today. Real progress. Couldn't he see his stubbornness would hurt her? This was too important to dismiss so quickly. She followed him into the shed and found him putting away the tools he and Caleb had been using. "Mr. Taylor, we need to finish our discussion."

He looked up, his eyebrows raised. "We weren't having a discussion."

"Well, I have a few things to say."

"You don't seem to understand. There is nothing to

discuss. I explained how things would be done and that's that."

She drew in a deep breath and said a prayer that she wouldn't lose her job on the first real day of teaching. "No, it's not."

"She's under my care and I determine what she should learn. You simply teach it."

"I see. I simply teach it." She struggled to keep her voice low. She wanted to polish that righteous expression right off his face. "And just how do I manage that when I can't tell what she's thinking?"

"That's a problem, isn't it?" Stuart calmly resumed organizing his tools. "Hannah and I seem to do all right. I know you'll work it out."

Her temper snapped. "How can you be so close-minded? You're stopping me even before I've started. She must learn to communicate in some way. With this, we meet her in the middle. It's her only alternative. Writing she simply does not comprehend yet."

Slowly he put the hammer he held onto the work-bench. His voice took on an edge of steel. "It's your job to teach her to comprehend it."

"Then you must support me in how I go about it."

She stared at him across the small room. She would not back down.

He pointed to the book. "Rachel, you can't be serious. No one else understands this kind of talk. She'll look like a fool."

His use of her given name jolted her. She liked the sound of it in his deep baritone voice. For a moment she lost track of the point she was trying to make. "Not to me. And not to you either if you learn the words. Are you more worried you will look the fool? Is that what you're afraid of?"

He scowled and she pressed home her point.

"She could teach you. That would help her learn, too. Then you could actually have a conversation with her. Don't you wonder what goes on in her head? What she's thinking?" She persisted in spite of the doubts she had of her own ability to teach Hannah all the words. What if she couldn't do it? Still, she needed his support, for Hannah to have any chance at all. There had to be some way to make him understand. "It would make her feel important."

He walked up to her and stood towering over her. Even though she knew it was a tactic to press home his authority, she still took an involuntary step backward.

"Enough," he said. "That is my answer. I won't pursue this further and I won't change my mind. The hand signs stop now."

How could she have ever thought he would understand? The camaraderie she had witnessed earlier when he worked with Caleb obviously didn't extend to her. "I don't know why I expected you to be different. You're just like any other man, blinded to any thoughts but your own." Trembling with fury, she continued. "Why don't you ask her what she wants? She'd tell you, but of course you wouldn't understand her anyway."

His jaw dropped open at her tirade and then clamped shut. She'd lose this job for sure now. Whirling about, she marched through the door.

She walked until she could go no farther, to the very

tip of the peninsula, struggling to calm her chaotic thoughts. She'd made a proper fool of herself. Her cheeks burned with the thought. Of course an adult shouldn't ask a child what they should learn. What was she thinking to say such a thing? She was grasping at wisps of thoughts—anything to make her point.

In front of her the ground dropped away sharply to the sea. Picking up a rock, she threw it over the edge, watching it bounce and ricochet off the angles of the cliff. She felt like that rock right now.

As it disappeared from sight a chill blew through her. That could have been Benjamin! The thought stopped her anger cold. She backed away from the edge and took a deep breath, remembering the picnic and the screams of a brave little boy. It would have been impossible for Caleb to save Benjamin. He would have died in the attempt had Mr. Taylor not insisted upon climbing down himself. She owed him a debt of gratitude even though he didn't want to accept it.

What was she doing arguing with him? Her purpose here was to teach. Perhaps that was why he upset her so. The signing had been her only plan and without it she didn't know what to do. Maybe she couldn't help Hannah at all. The thought scared her.

She turned back to the lighthouse and stopped. Mr. Taylor watched her from the doorway. She took a deep breath. He'd soon learn she could be stubborn—as stubborn as him, if need be. And she would figure something out, some way to reach Hannah. This entire argument was just a challenge to her to be more creative, that's all.

She marched up the lighthouse steps. "Hannah and Caleb are too quiet."

Their hands grabbed the brass door handle at the same time. His skin burned against hers for a moment before she snatched her hand away, unable to hide the turmoil he caused in her.

"We'll sort this out, Miss Houston," he said quietly.

He stood so close she could feel his breath on her neck. She glanced up into his blue eyes and saw the concern there. All she could comprehend was that he had not called her Rachel, and for some reason that hurt.

He yanked open the wooden door, standing aside for her to enter.

"Rach! Come look at this!" Caleb called from the parlor. A rectangular slash of orange sunlight fell upon him and Hannah kneeling before a small opened trunk.

"We need to start home," she said, acutely aware of the man behind her. His presence seemed to fill the room.

Caleb tossed something small across the space to her.

She caught it and turned it over. "What's this?" A wood carving. She ran her fingers over the smooth grain, taking a moment to gather her senses before turning to Mr. Taylor. With effort, she kept her voice light. "So, is this what light keepers do on long winter nights?"

He seemed wary of her mood. "The boat, many years ago. When I was Caleb's age."

"And this?" She picked up another carving. "The whale?"

"Last year."

"You had a bit of trouble with the tail?"

"It's not broken." He opened his mouth to say more, but stopped and turned to Caleb. "You heard your sister. Time to go."

Caleb slipped something into his pocket and closed the trunk. Rachel was about to ask him what he had in his hand when he pointed to the top of the trunk and asked, "This you, Mr. Taylor?"

Rachel leaned closer. The initials "M.S.T." had been burned into the wooden lid just above the words: "Lansing Enterprises."

"I'll tell you what," Mr. Taylor said. "You keep your secrets and I'll keep mine."

Chapter Nine

Stuart found a level spot on the large flat boulder and sat, motioning for Caleb to do the same. He'd wanted to escape the lighthouse and the lesson. Fishing was the perfect answer. Rachel gave her best as a teacher, and Hannah seemed happy to learn anything—anything with the exception of the alphabet. After three weeks of struggling, Stuart didn't know who was more frustrated—Rachel or Hannah.

Beside him, Caleb pulled an extra length of string from his pocket and cut the frayed end with an old knife that Stuart recognized as one of his. Caleb added more string to his line, deftly tying a fisherman's knot.

Stuart held up the string. "You know something of fishing." He didn't miss the flash of pride that Caleb quickly covered up. "You can swim, right?"

Caleb nodded.

"That's good," he said, looking down at the swells that crawled up the rock, then crashed back into themselves seven feet below them. The swells continued toward shore on either side of the rock, growing into white foaming cliffs that raced onto the beach behind Stuart.

He placed the can of bait between them on the dark-gray rock. They baited and then threw in their lines. A comfortable silence fell between them as the sun warmed their shoulders.

Stuart wondered how the teaching session was going. To Rachel's credit, she'd played by the rules—his rules. He hadn't expected such stubbornness the first time they'd talked. Now he knew better. His only experience with women had been his mother, Linnea and her mother, Rose. They'd been sweet and yielding to the men in their lives. He chuckled to himself. Nothing like Rachel.

He glanced sideways at Caleb. "I think this is preferable to being in the way while your sister tutors."

Caleb grinned. "You mean safer, don't you? I don't know what you did to make her mad, but you better watch your back."

"She doesn't have to like me. She just has to do right with Hannah." He started to say more but Caleb's line went taut.

"Think I got one!"

"Careful." Stuart stood, ready to lend a hand if need be. "Slow and easy."

Caleb worked the fish, allowing it a little line and then reeling it in with a steady hand. He landed the fish at his feet. "A sand bass!"

Stuart grabbed the line above the squirming, flopping fish, took it firmly by the gills and removed the hook from its mouth. He walked over to a shallow natural pool in the rock and slipped the bass down into it. "That'll make a nice supper for you."

"If I can get Rach to fix it. She hates fish."

"I could teach you, I guess." In answer to Caleb's questioning look he added, "To clean it and cook it up."

"Ah, I know how to do all that."

"Good. Then you don't need to bother your sister with it."

"Are you crazy? Why should I do it when she is supposed to? It's her job. I'm not doing woman's work."

He settled back on the rock and threw his line. "You eat the fish don't you? Then you can clean and cook them just as easy as she can."

"Why do it when she will if I just wait her out?"

Stuart bit back a smile that threatened. He couldn't fault Caleb's logic, but he also couldn't abide laziness. "Guess you do need watching, just like the sheriff said."

"Now wait one minute!"

"Your actions give you away. You figure it out."

At sixteen, Stuart had been by all counts a man. Dorian had seen to it he had not had one moment of idle time, making him work as a hand on one of his merchant ships. Perhaps that's why he enjoyed the odd friendship with Caleb, the endless questions—so many that he wondered if Caleb got much of a chance to voice his opinions around home. He had finally realized why the boy seemed so familiar. The red hair should have alerted him sooner. Caleb had been the one to steal his lobster.

"So who is this Enrique you run with? The one with the boat."

Caleb shrugged.

"A friend?"

"He's okay."

Silence followed, but a red line crept up Caleb's neck.

"How long have you known?" Caleb asked in a low voice.

"Awhile."

The boy's shoulders slumped. "You gonna tell my sister?"

Stuart shook his head. "No, but I want my trap back."

Caleb nodded. "It was a dare." Suddenly he sat up straight. "I can't believe you took a shot at us! What'd ya do that for? You scared the pee right out of me."

Stuart struggled to keep from smiling. "You're lucky I wasn't feeling meaner."

Caleb's eyes narrowed. "You wouldn't have hurt us."

"No. I just wanted to scare you off. The shots worked. I've never seen anyone row as hard as you and that friend of yours."

He pointed across the water to a long boat riding the swells. "Whalers. I'm surprised they got one so early in the season. Didn't expect to see any migrating for another two or three weeks."

The vessel drew nearer, hauling the carcass of a gray whale about forty feet long. Barnacles covered patches of the skin and blood clotted at the blowhole.

"Town will stink for days now," Caleb said, his nose wrinkling.

They stayed until they each had two fish, then

Stuart stood and gathered his things. "We better head back. I want to see how the tutoring is going and you've got fish to clean."

At the top of the trail, Stuart handed off his pole to Caleb with instructions to put them away and get started cleaning the fish behind the shed. He walked to the house, mentally bracing himself for another battle of wills with Miss Houston regarding Hannah. He had to commend her perseverance though. And thankfully, she hadn't resorted to tears to get her way.

The scene in the kitchen brought him up short.

Hannah, a towel tied around her waist, stirred a large bowl of dough at the table. The determined look on her face amused him—and made him proud. Rachel chopped squares of chocolate into smaller bits and added them to the stiff dough. When he stepped into the room, she stopped with the knife in midair. Brushing wisps of burnished hair off her face with the back of her hand, she dared him with her look to remark about her teaching method this time.

But it was the smell he couldn't get enough of. He hadn't had cookies since he was a boy. He couldn't breathe deep enough to take in the wonderful aroma of them baking. He felt almost foolish, standing there, simply breathing.

Rachel glanced at her brother, who'd entered behind Stuart.

"Any luck?"

Caleb nodded. "I need a bowl to put the cleaned fish in. Hey! Cookies! Any for us?"

"Over there." She motioned with a wooden spoon.

"Wash your hands first, though. I don't want them smelling like fish. We baked sugar cookies first. These are taking a little longer. Hannah measured the ingredients just fine but mixing them has slowed her down."

Rachel held up her cookbook and tapped the recipe with the spoon. "In case you don't approve," she directed the remark to Stuart, "I'll have you know Hannah read all of the amounts correctly after the first few tries."

Stuart acknowledged the jab by raising his brows. He knew when to keep quiet. Besides—this is more what he had in mind in the way of teaching—much more. This was practical. Something Hannah could always use. "I doubt you were able to find all you needed in my cupboard. What do I owe you?"

"Nothing. I'll take some of the cookies home for us." She stopped dropping spoonfuls of dough onto the baking sheet. "You didn't have much in your cupboard. Is there anything I can bring from town to save you a trip? Perhaps some fruit?"

"No. You are doing enough." He walked over to Hannah and lightly squeezed her arm. "I didn't know making cookies required such muscles."

Hannah crinkled her eyes with delight, but Rachel looked at him as if she couldn't believe he had actually teased. Guess he had been gruff with her, but it was best to keep his distance.

"Can I have a taste?" Caleb asked, leaning over Hannah's shoulder and hooking a finger of stiff dough.

"May I…" Rachel corrected. "Now out of here." She looked pointedly at Stuart. "Both of you."

He wasn't about to let her have the upper hand. "You have flour on your nose, Miss Houston."

"Oh." Her hand flew to her face, patting more flour in the same place and making her sneeze.

He stifled a grin. "Here. I'll do it." He grabbed a towel from the table and gently wiped the flour off the side of her nose and cheek. Her skin had darkened to a golden sun-kissed tan since her first visit to the peninsula, and she still had those cute freckles across the bridge of her nose that reminded him of a schoolgirl. "How old are you, Miss Houston? All of sixteen?"

Suddenly he became aware of how she watched him. Acutely aware. Her gaze lighted on his face, his scar, his mouth and everywhere her gaze touched, he tingled. She didn't breathe. Her lips parted.

And his heart stopped.

Slowly he drew the towel away and studied her face, the soft rounded line of her chin, her straight nose. Her green eyes sparkled with life. The urge to kiss her slammed into him. Her lips looked so soft, so yielding. He took a deep breath.

Watch yourself, Taylor. You don't deserve someone like her. You don't deserve anyone at all.

"Finish those before you head home," he said. "We'd just burn what was left." He tossed the towel at her. "Oh…and next time you come? Wear a hat. You're getting freckles."

Chapter Ten

San Francisco, November 1873

Dorian Lansing's ornate carriage pulled by two large black horses jostled toward the pier. On the dock, sailors unloaded wares from the large cutters and steamers. A sweaty beggar, carrying the stench of the streets, brushed past the carriage. Dorian remained aloof, ignoring the curious stares of the common people and his fellow merchants alike.

His wife sat beside him, a scented handkerchief daintily pressed to her nose. He seldom brought her here to his place of business. Ever since the accident the ships and the commotion unnerved her. However, information had finally arrived—news of their grand-daughter, and Rose had wanted to come with him. Dorian rapped his black cane on the carriage's ceiling when they neared his ship, the *Rose*.

"Here, Johnson."

The coach lurched to a stop and the driver jumped down and placed a stepping stool at the door. Dorian assisted his wife out and tucked her hand in the crook of his arm. He tightened his grip on his cane. This place festered with ruffians but he would keep her safe.

They walked up the ship's gangplank to the deck where his captain waited, stiff and formal. "Greetings, sir, ma'am. You'll find everything in order." ⋅

"Productive voyage, I trust?"

"Yes, sir. As usual."

"Well done."

He had few worries where Captain Ross was concerned. The man had been in his employ for seventeen years and had faithfully seen to his duty. A shame he hadn't been captain of the *Frisco Maiden* on her last voyage. Dorian had no doubt the man would have salvaged the vessel, not to mention Dorian's own daughter and granddaughter. Matthew had sailed often with Captain Ross, but experience and wisdom are not one and the same, and Matthew had lacked in the latter. "Where is Mr. Pittman?"

"My quarters, sir."

Dorian nodded, dismissing the captain to his duties, and led his wife to the quarters on the foredeck. He tapped firmly on the oak door with his cane. The door opened and a short mouse of a man peered out through thick glasses.

"Ah! Mr. Lansing. I thought I might see you upon docking."

He looked over to scrutinize Rose and then back to his boss.

"She did fine with arithmetic and the cooking."

"But not spelling, not words." Mortified at the whine in her voice, she struggled to take hold of her emotions. "Please, please, reconsider your decision about the signing."

Stuart's eyes hardened. "That subject is closed."

"Then maybe this teacher has had it." Her chest tightened with defeat. She had to look away from the troubled expression on his face. He expected too much, wanted too much from her.

"You don't mean that. You are not a quitter."

She didn't trust herself to answer him, afraid she'd burst into tears and make a complete fool of herself. Right now she felt like a quitter. She couldn't teach—at least not someone as complicated as Hannah. What had ever given her the notion that she could? She threw her cloak over her shoulders, preparing to head back to town.

Mr. Taylor stepped closer. "You're giving up? Leaving?"

"People leave," she said in low voice, thinking of her father and Joseph.

"You've been at this for five weeks and I know it hasn't been easy. What you and Hannah need is a holiday."

She stared at him. He'd never shown one ounce of caring about her feelings. Surely his concern was only for his daughter. If Rachel quit, he'd have to find another tutor.

"Let's go down to the water. I need to work on my boat. We'll take a picnic."

The offer sounded stiff on his lips, so stiff Rachel had

to turn away from him to the cupboard to hide the smile that suddenly threatened.

"What do you say?" he persisted.

He wasn't used to asking for anything, she realized, inanely flattered that he'd felt compelled to stop her. Her resolve to leave ebbed. "All right. I'll pack a few things. *You* can deal with Hannah."

Fifteen minutes later, she stepped from the lighthouse and tugged her cloak about her shoulders. On the footpath, scruffy brush snagged her skirt and loose gravel made the going slippery. Enviously she noted Stuart's canvas pants and loose muslin shirt that offered him freer movement. Even his cap stayed on better in the wind than her hood. With his toolbox in his right hand, he shifted the weight of the rolled quilt under his left arm, making her sharply aware of the long line of his powerful back, and headed down the path ahead of her.

As though he could read her thoughts, he stopped suddenly and turned, waiting for her to catch up to him. Then without a word, he started down the path again, this time at a slower pace.

Two hundred feet ahead, Caleb and Hannah raced on the narrow strip of beach, their footprints dotting the wet sand. They skirted the ocean-smoothed boulders and jagged rocks that jutted out into the water, stopping every few feet to dig for the sand crabs that washed up on the beach. Caleb yelled triumphantly when he caught the first one, showed it to Hannah, then with a quick overhand arc tossed it back into the surf.

Rachel turned her attention back to the end of the trail, watching Stuart jump effortlessly down the three-foot drop-off to the sandy beach. Her descent would be anything but graceful in her full skirt. She handed him the picnic basket and had crouched down when the warm press of his fingers against her sides surprised her.

A tingling awareness shot through her.

He set her firmly on the sand, then started up the beach. Was it just the tug and pull of her own emotions that she felt? Ever since the day she'd baked cookies with Hannah he had confused her. One minute he'd be almost friendly, then the next as distant as the ships on the horizon, which was an attitude she could barely tolerate. She preferred even his grouchy moments to being ignored. Picking up the basket again, she hurried after him, trying to match his long stride.

"I'll check on the boat first," he said without looking back.

The gritty sand quickly worked its way into her shoes and stockings, slowing her down. The sides of her feet were rubbed raw in less than fifty steps.

Turning to wait for her, Stuart frowned. "Take off your shoes."

Her cheeks warmed. "It's not proper. What kind of example would I set for Hannah if I did that?"

"You're ruining them. Besides, I expect a healthy dose of common sense to go along with Hannah's education."

"But," she said, weakly, and then sighed. Why argue? He was right.

She motioned Stuart to turn his back, then sat down

on a nearby boulder and removed her shoes and stockings. When she glanced up and caught him spying, she stood abruptly, letting her dress rustle into place.

He ignored her discomfort and stared at her feet. Then slowly his gaze moved up the length of her to her face, leaving behind a trail of tingles. "It has been a long time since I walked barefoot with a beautiful girl."

Her mouth dropped open.

He picked up her shoes and handed them to her, pausing a moment before turning and heading up the beach.

She dug her toes into the sand, trying to concentrate on the grainy feeling against her skin rather than the rapid thudding of her heart.

Beautiful?

Bemused, she followed at a slower pace.

A short way farther, he ducked inside a tarp-covered lean-to. Curious, Rachel peeked inside. The faint odor of fresh paint stung her nostrils. A neat array of coiled ropes and equipment lay in the bed of the ten-foot whitewashed dory.

The boat seemed small to Rachel. "This is what you go out in?"

He reached for a piece of sandpaper. "She's fit. Rescued enough stranded fisherman in her day to prove her worth."

She'd avoided thinking about the dangerous part of his job. How could he risk his life when Hannah depended totally on him? Why didn't he take a safer job? Rachel didn't understand him, and that made her more curious than ever. She wouldn't pry. Their friendship—if that's what it was—was too fresh, too new. But she'd find out eventually. Of that she was sure.

He bent to his work using exacting, swift strokes of the sandpaper. He tested an area for smoothness, then, dissatisfied, returned to sanding, moving into a rhythm—back and forth, back and forth. The muslin shirt pulled across his broad shoulders, and she thought how strong and able he was. How pleasant it might feel to have him sliding his hands over her instead of the boat. As soon as the thought registered, she felt her cheeks flush.

Before long the furrows of tension in his brow disappeared, and a sheen of sweat glossed his forehead. He paused and removed his cap, wiping his brow with his forearm.

She broke her stare. "I'll...go and lay out the quilt." She ducked through the tarp's open flap, breathing easier once out in the fresh air.

She busied herself spreading the quilt and anchoring it with the picnic basket. The early-morning overcast had burned off, and the sun warmed the beach. She removed her cloak and tossed it on the quilt, and then she walked to the water's edge where Hannah and Caleb played.

A short while later, Stuart joined her.

"The boat?"

"I finished what I came to do. She'll need another coat of paint but that's work for another day."

Rachel felt him staring and because it made her feel odd to be studied so closely, she turned her attention to the surf pounding against the rocks. "This was a good idea."

"You are a good teacher—an excellent one. Don't be discouraged."

His words warmed her. "I might not be discouraged at all if you'd let me try the signing." But she knew he wouldn't and kept her voice light, cajoling.

He shook his head. "Let it alone, Rachel. You never give up, do you?"

She smiled sweetly. "Not when I'm right. I'm just trying to use that common sense that you so want Hannah to learn."

"You can't wear me down," he warned.

"I know." She turned to meet his gaze, serious now. "I wouldn't think much of a man who didn't hold to his convictions. As much as you oppose my position, I still respect yours and the fact that you feel strongly about it."

A slow smile spread across his tanned face. "Good. Then we'll get along."

Rachel's heart beat faster. The twinkle in his eyes was entirely too interesting. *Common sense,* she told herself. This was a business relationship, nothing more. "It strikes me that you are always taking care of things—Hannah, the boat, the light." And her. Today she'd been ready to quit teaching, feeling like a failure. He'd known somehow that she needed a break, needed to step back.

"The light?" He shrugged his shoulders. "That's my job. The boat? It helps me do my job."

"And Hannah…"

"Hannah. Well…Hannah is my responsibility."

"Ouch! I'm glad she isn't close enough to hear that,"

Rachel said. What a strange way to think of his daughter. But the love was there in the way he treated her. "What happened with her, Stuart? How did she lose her voice? Or—" she paused as the thought occurred to her "—has she never been able to speak?"

He picked up a smooth stone and skimmed it over the water.

She watched it arc two, three, four times before dropping underneath the surface. "Well? Are you stalling?"

He let out a huff of breath, avoiding her gaze.

"Perhaps it would help me to know. In order to teach her better."

A slight smile played about his mouth. "I doubt that. I guess you're entitled though. You've put a lot of effort into her lessons. And as much as it may have pained you, you have followed my wishes."

"Which has been the hardest part of all," she teased.

He started walking slowly along the shore and she kept pace with him. Suddenly he stopped and faced her. "Let there be a bargain. I'll tell you about Hannah, but then you have to tell me something about you."

She pursed her lips.

"Ah, I see. Turnabout is fair play, Miss Houston."

She scowled. He was almost charming. Had she misread the awkwardness at the lighthouse? "But my life is ever so boring."

"We'll see about that," he said, cocking his head. "I won't say a word until you agree."

"This sounds suspiciously like blackmail."

He smirked. "You're the one who mentioned there

were rumors about me. I wouldn't want to disappoint you."

"Well, so far, Mr. Taylor, you have been anything but disappointing. Exasperating, yes. Disappointing, no."

He smiled, and it transformed his face.

She thought his chest puffed out a little, too. "You go first, then."

He nodded, his mood changing swiftly to serious. "When Hannah was three, her mother drowned in a ship accident at sea. Hannah hasn't spoken since."

Rachel had heard of such things…of being so traumatized that blindness or deafness occurred without a physical reason for it. "Has she seen a doctor?"

"I took her to a specialist up the coast."

"And…?" she prodded. "What did he say?"

"He said that she'll speak again. Someday."

His words didn't exactly answer Rachel's question, and she suspected there was much more to the story, but the fact that he'd trusted her with this much would do for now.

"Your turn now." Stuart skimmed another stone over the water. "Obviously by your accent you are not from here."

"La Playa is filled with strange accents—Spanish, Portuguese, Chinese. Compared to those, a Midwest one isn't too exotic."

"True enough, but yours is pleasant. Go on."

"Remember, it's quite boring," she warned.

"I doubt that."

She groaned, but was warmed by the fact that he was interested. "When I was fourteen my mother died from the influenza and my father came west. Caleb and I followed him from camp to camp looking for gold. We moved here in '70 when he heard that gold had been discovered in the back country."

Stuart nodded. "I remember hearing of that."

"After a few years, he was ready to move again, but I had had enough. I was tired of the dirt and fleas and roughness of the tent cities. I wanted a real home, with a roof over my head that didn't leak. I heard La Playa was looking for a schoolteacher, so I applied for the position and then came to stay with Reverend Crouse and his wife."

"That's it?"

She buried a shell deep into the soft sand with her toe. "Pretty much."

"You're what—twenty-three at most? In all these tent cities there were no suitors? No one special?"

Her cheeks flushed. How could he fluster her so easily? She couldn't tell him about Joseph. Joseph who'd captured her heart and then nearly destroyed it when he'd left. "I'm a few years beyond that," she admitted. "You must be unaware of the power of gold. Once a man gets caught up in it, it takes hold of him and won't let go. Nothing is as important as chasing the next rumor of gold—not even a woman."

He scrutinized her. "So you came here."

She took a deep breath. "I'd rather be on my own, taking care of myself, than saddled to a man who would always put me second in his life behind gold."

Stuart looked at her strangely, and for a moment she thought her words had revealed more than she'd meant to.

"Papa promised he'd be back, but we haven't seen him since." When she looked up, the anger on Stuart's face surprised her. She couldn't understand what had upset him, so she hurried to explain. "We're doing just fine. I have a good job teaching. We're all right."

"But a man should take care of his family—not run off and leave them to their own fate."

"A nice thought, but hardly reality. People leave." Joseph had left her. Her voice lowered to barely a whisper above the roar of the waves. "Everyone leaves."

His brows knitted together as he frowned. "You don't really believe that, do you?"

"I have to. Caleb depends on me, at least for now, but one day he'll be gone too. More and more he talks of trying his hand at whaling. I can't afford to believe anything else." She didn't add that it would hurt too much to hope that someone would come along, someone who would care so much that he'd put her and her welfare before his ambition or dreams.

Stuart strolled along the beach, waiting when she stopped to examine a seashell. "What about Morley?"

"Terrance?" She looked into his blue eyes.

"The mercantile owner. You were with him at the picnic."

So he'd noticed that much and remembered. "He's just a friend."

"But he wants to be more."

She thought so, too, but wasn't ready to admit to it. She pulled her gaze from his and started walking again. "Enough about me. You know far more than I do about you."

He flashed a grin. "An employer's prerogative."

"Rach!" Caleb splashed through the shallows toward her. "Take a look at this!" He held a sand dollar in his palm.

She jumped back from the water spray, but was grateful for the distraction. "It's huge! Where did you find it?"

She followed her brother around a large boulder. Hannah crouched there next to a wet rocky crevice. She placed a shell in Rachel's hand. The shell moved!

"Oh!" Rachel nearly dropped it.

Stuart caught her hand in his, steadying her, and turned the shell over. "It won't hurt you. See? Just a hermit crab."

Rachel stilled, more aware of Stuart's warm touch than the tickling trail of the creature. "It just startled me." She dropped the crab back into the pool and found five more shells trundling along the sides of the rock. She squatted down and touched an unusual-looking sea flower that clung to the rock beneath the water's surface. The tentacle-like petals grasped onto her finger. "Oh!" Quickly, she pulled back.

"Sea anemone," Caleb said. "They always do that."

She frowned at Caleb, who grinned back at her.

"Now, that is a surprise," Stuart said with a bemused look. "I didn't take you for the skittish type."

"She doesn't like creepy-crawly things," Caleb said. "But she tries not to show it."

"Good idea not to let people know. They could use it against you," Stuart whispered into her ear. "Especially your brother."

"Exactly," she mumbled, her eyes shooting play

daggers at Caleb. "It doesn't help to pass along a silly fear to Hannah." She enjoyed watching the creatures in the tide pool—as long as they stayed there. "This must be where Hannah finds the things for the treasure box in her room."

"Too many if you ask me," Stuart said.

She rose to her feet. "It's a good way to keep memories."

"Memories," he murmured. "More a curse than anything."

She thought of her mother and father. The good and the bad. Of Hannah, now voiceless since the death of her mother. "Yes…they can be. But they make us who we are, whether we want them to or not."

Stuart's gaze met hers, but he didn't say anything more.

She followed him, picking her way over the rocks back to the beach. Once there she brushed the sand from her hands and looked around. To the south the large flat fishing rock walled her in and to the east and north, the cliffs. She pointed partway up the sandstone. "I can't believe that's the waterline."

"High tide."

"It changes so drastically. Where we are standing is underwater then."

A half smile moved across his face. "The pull of the moon is an amazing thing. The flood current—" he caught her questioning look "—high tide, comes in here fast. When it does, there is no place to reach the trail."

He stooped, choosing a stone, and in one fluid move, skimmed it across the shallow surf.

She watched, fascinated, as he repeated the motion. Strange though it would be to the people of La Playa, she liked talking with him. The sound of his deep voice rumbling on about tides and currents mesmerized her until she really didn't hear what he was saying, just enjoyed the sound.

The wind swirled within the sandstone cavern creating a haunting moan. She shivered and rubbed her arms, wishing for her cloak that she'd left behind on the quilt. "Funny how cold it gets as soon as we're out of the sun."

He glanced down at her arms encased in cotton sleeves. Light flashed through his eyes.

She shivered again. This time, not from the cold.

Slowly, as though he couldn't quite help himself, he reached out and rubbed her upper arms. Heat from his hands burned through the material to her skin. The fact that only an hour ago at the boat she'd dreamed of his touch shot through her mind.

"Rachel…" His voice rasped softly. She heard desire banked in it. He tightened his grip.

Her heart hammered in her chest. "My teacher's position doesn't cover this sort of thing."

"Oh, I'm sure there's a rule against it." His eyes were the bluest thing in creation, hooded now, pulling her in.

Common sense, she told herself. Use common sense. "Yes…I…" Yet she wanted his touch. It shook her to realize how much she suddenly yearned for it. But if she were to let him closer, he'd end up leaving her eventually. It was better not to let that happen, better to keep focused on her work. She took a deep breath and stepped from his grasp.

He stared at her a moment, then dropped his hands to his sides before shoving them in his pockets. "Let's go back with the others. You'll warm up faster in the sun."

She swallowed hard and watched him start back around the fishing rock, feeling the cold once again seep through her skin.

He glanced back once, stopped and faced her. "There's more to your story, Rachel. A lot more."

As he turned to leave, she raised her chin. "I could say the same about you, Mr. Taylor."

Chapter Twelve

Stuart climbed the circular stairs, his supplies for the lamp in one hand. At the top, he set the bucket on the plank flooring and unrolled his linen apron, following the lighthouse board instructions in rote manner, barely thinking of the actions he had done so many times over the past year.

In the distance the church bell rang out, calling those that would go to Sunday worship. There wouldn't be many, for most of the area's inhabitants were Portuguese or Mexican. They would go to the Catholic church in Old San Diego. Rachel would be sitting quietly. Caleb, on the other hand, would be fidgeting, anxious for the service to be over.

Thoughts of Rachel haunted him more and more lately. He looked forward to her visits, but when she arrived, he did his best to keep his distance, yet still found reasons to brush up against her or hold her as she climbed into and out of her carriage. Innocent yearnings—and yet not quite innocent.

The thought troubled him. He didn't want to like her.

And that situation at the beach…well, that was another thing entirely. Loneliness on his part perhaps, maybe lust. His monkish existence was getting to him. Having Rachel so near, and so beautiful, had undone him for a moment. He would have to be more careful from now on. She deserved better than him. She deserved someone with a future.

He blocked the faint tolling of the bell from his mind and continued his work. For him, Sunday was not a day of rest. It was just like any other day filled with the same monotonous yet necessary chores. He trimmed the wick to the required length and shape, remembering the precise shape the flame had to have upon burning, and then polished the carbon off the reflectors. The endless repetition of caring for the lamp was tedious.

He looked out to sea. A steamer headed toward the harbor, still far enough away that any persons on deck were indiscernible. The wind was mild, the water calm. He missed the ocean. He could say that now, although it hadn't always been that way. For the first two years after Linnea died, he'd hated it. Now he wondered if he would ever be able to go back.

When he finished with his chores he stored his equipment in the small storage space at the bottom of the inside ladder that led to the catwalk. He peeked in on Hannah. She sat in her bedroom, her back to the door, playing with the doll Rachel had given her. Dust motes circled around her head in the bright morning sunlight that streamed through the window.

She sat so still he grew curious. He stepped closer,

wondering that she could concentrate so hard and not hear him. Suddenly she flipped her hands about in a coordinated dance, and then tried to make the doll copy her. Suspicious now, he moved closer. A book lay open in her lap. A book with pictures and symbols.

"Hannah! What are you doing?" He strode to the bed and snatched the book from her.

Her eyes widened with fear. She should worry—she had disobeyed him.

"You may not do the hand signs!" He paced the length of the room, his anger growing with each step. "I can't believe Miss Houston left this for you. She knows how I feel about it."

Book in hand, he stomped down the stairs and paced the length of the gravel walk. He could wring Rachel's neck! How dare she encourage this in Hannah? He'd been sure that finally they were of the same accord on things—that trust was developing. Well, she'd see just how serious he was. They'd have this out once and for all.

He sat on the outside steps. Behind him, Hannah's footsteps sounded on the stairs, and then he felt the brush of her arm as she sat beside him. He hardened himself against the sight of tears on her wet spiky lashes.

"Go to your room."

She wouldn't look at him, instead she pointed to herself, and then crossed her arms over her chest.

"You are not allowed to use that. Dr. Jarvis said it was just a matter of time before you started talking again. Now go back upstairs."

Her chin quivered, but she didn't leave. She shoved the book he held toward him and repeated her motions.

"Hannah. It's for your own good. You will speak again one day. You just need time."

Determination sparked in her clear gray eyes. Stubborn determination.

Stuart swallowed. "I will punish you if I see you talking with your hands."

He hated being stern with her and cringed at the sound of his voice. Rachel had done this. Had driven this wedge into his relationship with Hannah—and she would pay for it.

Hannah pushed the book at him again, harder this time.

"All right," he said irritably. "I'll look this once." He flipped through the pages searching for the arms-crossed-over-the-chest picture. Finally, on one dog-eared page, he found it:

"I love you."

His heart jolted as he stared at the page. He drew in a deep, shuddering breath. Had he been such a fool? The book slipped from him, and he buried his face in his hands, trying to think beyond the lump in his throat. Hannah had never told him before. When she could talk, aboard the ship, she'd been too afraid of him, afraid of all men—a legacy left from her father.

He felt a tug on his sleeve.

Slowly he straightened. The words surged from deep inside him, rusty and awkward. "I…I love you too, Hannah."

She burrowed into his arms. For the first time since the accident, he felt a measure of peace.

* * *

Rachel and Caleb had been unable to come for more than a week. He wondered what had kept her away as he walked toward her now. The days were getting shorter and perhaps that left little time for her to tend to her other obligations in town. Well, once he had his say, she might have plenty of time. Suddenly he wasn't so anxious to put the coming confrontation behind him.

She stood by her carriage, hands splayed on hips. The brown skirt and cream-colored blouse made her look very "teacherly" as did the furrow between her brows. "What's wrong?"

He glanced toward the shed, checking for Hannah and Caleb.

Rachel's eyes narrowed. "They can't hear you."

Watching her, he couldn't believe she'd left the book on purpose. And yet what other explanation could there be? He couldn't let go of the notion that she'd gone behind his back to get her way. The thought had even robbed him of sleep. "I found the book."

"Book?" she said, a bewildered expression on her face.

"The signing book. Did you think I wouldn't find it eventually?" The anger that he'd pushed down inside forced its way up and flooded his voice. Even Jericho snorted and pranced sideways.

"Well," Rachel recovered quickly. "Good. I've been looking for it."

"Hannah has been practicing the gestures."

Amazement crossed Rachel's face, irritating him further. "Don't look so pleased."

She scowled. "What exactly are you accusing me of? I didn't leave the book with her."

"Then how did it end up here?"

Caleb rounded the side of the lighthouse with Hannah and glanced uneasily from Stuart to his sister. "What's going on? What's all the shouting about?"

Stuart ignored him. "My word has to mean something. And I specifically instructed you not to teach the signing." He swatted at the tug on his arm. "Hannah, stop pulling at my sleeve."

The instant she had his attention, Hannah started signing, her hands dancing in short jerky movements.

Stuart let out an exasperated grunt and turned to Rachel. "You are the expert. What is she saying?"

"I...I don't know. Hannah, slow down. Remember, I haven't learned all the words."

Hannah repeated her motions. When no one could understand, she dropped in a heap to the dirt. In her frustration, she began tearing out the sparse tufts of grass and throwing them angrily at the ground.

Rachel stared helplessly at Stuart.

He felt more than a twinge of guilt. All he'd been striving for was the truth. He hesitated. Maybe that wasn't the important thing here. Maybe the way Hannah had obtained the book didn't really matter— not anymore. What mattered was how he handled it from here on out.

"All right, Hannah. This seems to be very important to you. Get the book."

He ignored Rachel's quick glance of surprise at his words. Hannah's hands stilled, full of grass. Slowly she raised her head. Uncertainty filled her eyes. After all his bellowing about rules, she must think she hadn't heard right.

"I'll get it. Where is it?" Caleb asked.

"Kitchen table," Stuart said, his gaze still locked on Hannah.

Caleb dashed up the dirt path to the lighthouse. When he returned to the group, Stuart opened the book. "Now go ahead. But slowly this time."

From her seat in the dirt, Hannah ever so slowly began making one word at a time with her hands. Her fingers trembled, and once, she had to start over, but that determined look he'd come to know so well stole over her face and remained.

He flipped through the book, searching for the pictures of her motions. "I've got that. Next." He felt Rachel watching him closely throughout the exchange and kept waiting for the words "I told you so" to slip from her lips.

When Hannah finished, he closed the book with a thud and helped her up from the ground. "Thank you for being honest."

He let out his breath slowly and then looked at Rachel. "Apparently Hannah took the book from your carriage. I…I apologize for assuming it was you."

Rachel raised her brows but remained silent.

"About the signing…" He took a deep breath. "I want it to continue."

She looked dubious. "You're sure?"

"At this point, I'm not sure of anything." *Except you,* he wanted to say as he studied her upturned face. *I'm beginning to be very sure of how I feel about you.* But saying the words would only complicate his life. He couldn't offer her a future. He didn't have one.

Chapter Thirteen

Something changed over the next weeks between the four of them. Quickly, Hannah learned to connect the images in the book—the word, the picture and the hand motion. Now that they were aware of her thoughts, she became so much more a part of them. Stuart wondered why he'd ever fought against the idea of sign language. Any argument he had used now sounded hollow against the rush of joy he felt at knowing Hannah's thoughts.

Stuart watched Hannah at the water's edge, her tin bucket in hand, searching for shells. Caleb joined her, kicking up water and making her squeal. Behind him, Rachel called out, "Stuart, this looks like a good place."

That was another thing that had changed. Rachel no longer called him Mr. Taylor. He liked the way his name sounded on her lips.

With a snap of his wrists, he spread out the quilt, and before long Rachel and then Hannah joined him. Hannah rinsed the shells off in the bucket of water and laid them out to dry while Rachel set out the food. Whistling sharply, Stuart caught Caleb's attention and motioned him over to eat. Seagulls, drawn by the hope of an easy meal, scattered as he ran up.

"With any luck," Stuart said, winking at Hannah, "we'll see our whale today." He finished his apple and stretched back on the quilt, propping himself up with his elbows. He forced himself to concentrate on the swells rising and then crashing down, although the urge to study Rachel was more appealing. The ocean was safer.

"Haven't most of them passed by?" Rachel asked, popping a grape into her mouth.

He shook his head. "There's a special one Hannah and I watch for. Should be heading south any day now."

She eyed him skeptically. "Right. And how do you know it's the same whale?"

"What? Don't you believe me?" he said teasingly.

"No. I don't think I do." But the dimple gave her away. "You will have to prove it to me."

As he studied her full lips, he decided proving it the way he'd like might be dangerous. "A torn fluke. Someone harpooned her or perhaps a shark bit her. Whatever the case, she got away. We first saw her last March when she migrated north. She had a calf with her."

His answer seemed to satisfy her, then her eyes widened. "A torn fluke…like the carving you made?"

He smiled, pleased and a little surprised that she remembered. More than ten weeks had passed since that first day of tutoring.

Hannah finished her lunch, tugged on his hand and pointed to the tidal pools.

"You go on." He tweaked her nose and waited for her to take off. Caleb quickly followed.

Stuart glanced at Rachel—and then couldn't look away. If she'd just quit enjoying those grapes he might be able to think clearly. He studied her profile as she watched Hannah and Caleb dash toward the water.

"Here." She held out a cluster of grapes for him.

He shook his head. It wasn't food he was after. "Thank you for all your help with Hannah."

"I've enjoyed it, although a few moments have been challenging."

"I'd like to make those up to you." He inched closer to her. Dangerous or not, he wanted a taste of her. He reached out and tucked a loose strand of hair behind her ear.

The teasing smile on her lips slowly disappeared as she realized his intent. Her green eyes grew large.

"Come here, Rachel."

"This is not wise," she whispered, but she didn't pull back.

"Probably not." He hooked his hand behind her neck and pulled her to him. "But I think we both know it's time. Come here."

He met her lips tenderly, softly. Slowly he let go of her neck and she stayed there, her mouth moving under his, answering his need.

"Stuart…" she breathed into his mouth.

Gently he pressed for more, using his tongue to tickle the seam of her lips. They parted and tentatively she touched her tongue to his. A bolt of desire coursed through him.

She gasped and pulled back, staring at him as the color heightened on her cheeks. A moment passed before she finally spoke, her voice shaky. "I believe that more than made up for any rough moments with your daughter."

"That made up for a lot of things, but not every-thing." He leaned in for another kiss. There was a rush-ing sound in his ears that had nothing to do with the nearby waves crashing to shore. Then he felt her hand splay against his chest and hold him away.

"No. Stuart." A look of distress passed over her face as the pressure on his chest increased. "Why...why don't you tell me about your scar?"

"My scar?" What was she talking about? He couldn't get his mind off the kiss.

"Yes! How did it happen?" she said sharply. "Now, mind you, I expect a fascinating tale. There are so many rumors in town. Like the one about the mountain lion that attacked you. Then there's the one where you were shot fleeing from prison."

He still reeled from the kiss and wanted another one, but obviously she wasn't ready. She was babbling in her nervousness and that wasn't like her at all.

He raked his hand through his hair, wondering whether to be amused that so many stories were circu-lating about him or upset that his existence hadn't gone as unnoticed as he'd hoped.

"Although I have to wonder," she continued, "if you did have a criminal record, how you managed to get the job of light keeper."

She was talking so fast. Her words tumbling over each other. She was nervous, he realized. Of him.

"A friend helped me get this job. Man named Saunders."

"And the scar?"

"I got it when I was swimming. The stern of a lifeboat rammed into me." He shrugged. "Not that exciting."

"You really need to embellish that story if you expect it to entertain as well as the rumors." But there was a twinkle in her eyes again, and her breathing was back to normal as she wrapped her arms about her knees, smoothing her skirt.

"I never set out to be the one everyone talks about," he said under his breath, angry at the thought. "And I'd never hurt you, Rachel."

"I know that," she said softly. "I…I was just scared. That's all. Of myself."

That makes two of us.

He nodded slowly. "I see."

Rachel sat up straight. "Wait a minute. You said lifeboat—not just boat." Her gaze narrowed. "This happened during the storm, didn't it?"

"You aren't going to let this go, are you?" He'd learned that much about her stubbornness. Yet if she knew the worst about him, she'd want nothing to do with him. He couldn't let that happen.

"My schooner was to land at San Pedro—that's the port for the Pueblo de Los Angeles. Normally good weather, like this today, comes with the northwest wind. Southeasters bring the bad weather where heavy black clouds roll in." He swallowed hard, remembering. "But it was neither. It was freakish—coming out of the north-east, with the strangest sky I'd ever seen. It pushed us farther south. The ocean had a force all its own. We started taking on water and had to man the lifeboats. I went forward to help Saunders, my senior officer, cut the boat loose from some debris. Before I could get back to my seat, a wave swept Linnea and Hannah overboard."

"Oh, Stuart." Her teasing mood had evaporated.

He didn't want her pity. "I dove in. Amazingly I caught hold of them both. I kicked for the surface, but couldn't get any closer. Linnea must have known I was struggling—trying to save both her and Hannah. I wasn't going to let go of either of them. But then she let go. Linnea simply let go."

He waited for the bitterness and self-hate to come as it did after his dreams, but it didn't come. He just felt numb. "Ironic, isn't it? I must have rescued at least ten people since manning the light tower, yet I couldn't save Linnea."

"It sounds as though it wasn't your choice."

"Oh, I had a choice, all right" he said bitterly. "Let Hannah drown while I tried once more to find her mother, or take Hannah to the surface."

She stared at him through eyes clear and steady. "That's no choice at all. You did the only thing you could have done."

He wanted to believe her, but there was that small voice inside him that said if only he'd tried harder, if only he'd been stronger. "Linnea had a slight build, but she was strong. She had a fierce hold while sitting in the lifeboat. Why didn't she hold on like that just a little while longer?"

"So Linnea made the choice for you. Since she knew you did not have the strength to save both her and her daughter."

The thought had crossed his mind before. He'd been afraid to believe it.

Rachel scanned the horizon. "That was three years ago, Stuart. How long do you plan to punish yourself?" she turned back to face him. "Don't you see? You've proven yourself by the way you've honored Linnea's memory. You've done a good job with Hannah. It's time to let it go, to forgive yourself. I'm sure Linnea would want that."

He stood and walked away a few paces. He couldn't accept this absolution she offered. She still didn't know the half of it—not about the murder, or the fact that Hannah wasn't even his child. "You don't understand. It was my ship. My responsibility. I've known the sea all my life, known the pull of the tides like they were inside me. Linnea should have been safe. It was my fault she died." *A man takes care of his own.*

While Caleb handled the reins on the bumpy ride back to town, Rachel sat next to him and contemplated what she had learned that day. The scar on Stuart's forehead was nothing compared to the scar on his heart. That one hadn't healed—might never heal. The rumors in town were wrong. He wasn't a fugitive from justice, he was a fugitive from himself. He couldn't forgive himself for Linnea's death.

In his unguarded moments, Rachel had caught a

glimpse of what he must have been like before he lost his wife. It scared her how desperately she wanted him to be like that again.

She buried her face in her hands as the thought came to her. She loved him! *Oh, Lord help her, she loved him.*

Chapter Fourteen

A brisk November breeze bit into Stuart's face while he looped Blanco's reins over the hitching rail in front of the mercantile and helped Hannah down. He took her hand and stepped onto the boardwalk, his gaze drawn across the square to the parsonage where Rachel lived. He felt a sudden tug on his hand and glanced down at Hannah. A question burned in her eyes.

"No. I'm sure they are busy. Besides, it will be dark soon." Her shoulders slumped and he almost smiled at the sluggish gait she assumed. He felt the same way. He couldn't block Rachel from his mind. Constantly he wondered what she was doing. An unfamiliar twinge of jealousy shot through him as he thought of her visiting with friends and neighbors, going on about her daily life here in town—especially her relationship with Morley.

How he wished he didn't have to deal with that man today. But his was the only mercantile between here and Old San Diego. He had no choice.

Two large barrels full of apples propped open the double doors to the shop. A tall woman in a dark dress stood behind the counter, her back to him as she reached for a jar of peppermint sticks on the highest shelf. She could just touch the jar, pushing it away from her when she probed for it.

"I'll get that for you," Stuart said.

At his voice, the woman spun around, a relieved look on her face. "Thank you. I would not bother you, but the step stool broke this morning."

"No trouble, ma'am." He walked around the end of the counter, took the jar from the shelf and handed it to her. Her cool fingers touched his a second longer than necessary. Still, she drew back and her eyes widened when she caught sight of his scar.

"Elizabeth!" Terrance strode through the doorway from the back storeroom. A scowl darkened his face when he saw Stuart.

Elizabeth jumped back at his voice, and Stuart noticed her resemblance in mannerism and height to the clerk, but where Terrance's brown eyes were suspicious and beady, hers held a friendly warmth. "Is there something I can help you with today, sir?"

"A few supplies for the lighthouse. I'll need a receipt to give to the board." He drew a folded piece of paper from his pocket and handed it to her.

"What lovely printing," Elizabeth said, her gaze moving from him to Hannah. "Here, dear." She handed Hannah a peppermint stick. "Because your father was so nice to help me." Looking back at Stuart she said, "I'll get these things directly."

Stuart relaxed slightly. He squeezed Hannah's hand and began to look about the store.

"Please don't handle the items unless you plan to purchase them," Terrance said. "And keep hold of that girl of yours."

Coldness washed through Stuart as Terrance stepped closer. Stuart met his stare with a measuring one of his own.

"You had mail this week." Terrance retrieved an envelope from his desk and slapped it on the counter. "We'll be getting mail drops more often now that the U.S. Army is moving to Ballast Point."

Stuart had seen the soldiers at the whaling station. "What of the Johnson Company?"

"They have to leave. Just as well, I guess. The whales are hunted out."

Outside, hard footsteps fell on the boardwalk as somebody ran by the front of the store, stopped and tripped back to the doorway.

"Caleb," Elizabeth called, shaking her finger at him. "You better get home. Your sister was here not fifteen minutes ago looking for you."

The boy ignored Elizabeth's warning. Instead he walked over to Hannah, hunkered down and tugged on the white ribbon sash from her navy blue dress. "Hey! Where's the dance?"

Hannah smiled, dropped Stuart's hand and signed something to Caleb.

"Whoa! You can't be ahead of me on your sand dollar collection. I don't believe you."

Hannah nodded, pure superiority shining from her face.

"Well, maybe…" He scratched his head as though perturbed. "I have a surprise at my house. Want to come?" He glanced at Stuart for permission.

At the thought of seeing Rachel, hope pulsed unexpectedly through Stuart. He turned to Elizabeth—her finger rested halfway down the piece of paper—then nodded to Caleb. "I'll collect her when I'm finished here."

"Come on, Hannah. I'm late. Bye, Miss Morley." Caleb raised a hand in farewell to Elizabeth who had stopped to watch the exchange. He tore out of the shop and dashed down the street with Hannah in tow.

A stunned look crossed Elizabeth's face. "My! I don't remember ever seeing Caleb so…so… He actually teased your daughter!"

Terrance walked up to the counter in front of Stuart. "You and Caleb seem to know each other quite well. Funny, I don't remember you speaking with him much at the picnic."

Stuart matched Terrance's hard stare but didn't enlighten him. What Caleb and he did with their time wasn't Morley's business.

"Hurry up, Elizabeth." Terrance tossed the words over his shoulder. "I'm sure he needs to get home before dark. You aren't supposed to leave the lighthouse, are you? There's a rule to that effect."

The challenge in Terrance's words was unmistakable.

Stuart turned away from the taunting. Elizabeth

hastened to fetch his supplies, her movements nervous and flighty. Terrance had her jumping to his every mood. How could Rachel think for a minute she would be happy with this man? He could barely stand the thought of him treating her as he did his sister.

Stuart strode to the far side of the room. A slow burn built inside at the way the man manipulated people. Terrance wouldn't have lasted long on one of Dorian's ships. He'd have been food for the sharks. Stuart glanced down at the letter in his hands. The writing was familiar. It was not signed, but he knew it was from Saunders: "Had a visitor yesterday. Lots of questions. He's still looking. Best to take note. S."

Saunders could easily talk a man into a comatose state, but when it came to writing, his letters were short—and few and far between at that. Stuart let out a long breath. Dorian was still searching for Hannah—and him.

When would that man give up? Had the time come for him and Hannah to move on? Stuart could think of only one reason to stay—Rachel.

"What's that your girl does with her hands?" Terrance said, pulling Stuart back to his surroundings.

Hadn't Rachel told him? He thought for sure she would have.

Elizabeth cleared her throat. "Anything else, Mr. Taylor?"

At the shake of his head, she pushed the slatted box of supplies toward his side of the counter. He paid quickly and, under the skeptical eye of Morley, carried the box to his horse. One by one he settled the apples and other items into his saddlebags, distributing the weight evenly. He started back into the store to return the box, but stopped short at the sound of heated voices coming from inside.

Elizabeth's voice rose. "All I have to say is that you had better watch yourself. If Rachel is meeting with that child as you suspect, she's also seeing him. You'd better make up your mind between her and Amanda."

"She wouldn't do that to me. Not Rachel. She has more class than that."

"Open your eyes. She's a woman. And a very independent one."

Stuart dropped the box by the doorway and strode to his horse. Hadn't Rachel mentioned her work to anyone? If Terrance and his sister were suspicious of her comings and goings, did the whole town wonder? Why had she kept it a secret? But he knew the answer to that—she'd lose her job without a doubt. The school board wouldn't stand for her visiting a single man and his girl.

Maybe he'd been wrong to ask her to tutor.

He glanced back at the lighted mercantile, watching Elizabeth's silhouette as she pulled the blinds. He'd lived for so long without a thought for anyone but himself and Hannah that he'd conveniently continued that way after Rachel and Caleb started coming to the lighthouse. He hadn't given any thought to the complications it might add to Rachel's life—the gossip, the speculation.

Until now....

People could be cruel. Just look at the way they'd treated Hannah. Why did he think they'd be any nicer to Rachel? They would circle like sharks the minute they sensed blood.

The mercantile door closed with a bang, shattering Stuart's thoughts. The store's lamps were out. Terrance locked the door and followed his sister down the board-walk, their footsteps echoing loudly until the sound died away into the stillness of twilight. That weasel Terrance didn't deserve Rachel.

But then…neither did he.

The strong aroma of bean soup filtered out into the night air as he led Blanco toward the parsonage. He heard voices coming from the back of the house. He tied Blanco's reins to a large saltbush and walked into the backyard.

A big black dog poked her nose out of the carriage house doorway and watched him. Behind her a small chorus of whining and yipping started up. The sound of whispers came from the shadowed building. A moment later Caleb emerged with Hannah at his side. Both of them carried a whimpering bit of black fluff. Hannah grinned at Stuart.

"Be careful of the pup's teeth, Hannah," Rachel warned from behind him. "They're sharp, like little cactus needles."

He spun around. She stood on the back house steps, wiping her hands on her apron. The way her sleeves were rolled up, he must have caught her in the middle of cooking supper. She looked hot, disheveled and beauti-ful. The urge to kiss her swept over him like a tidal wave.

Behind her Reverend Crouse cleared his throat. Rachel stiffened at the sound. And in that moment

Stuart realized she hadn't said a word to anyone about her trips to the lighthouse.

He nodded, shoving his hands into his pockets. "Miss Houston…Pastor. Cute pups. How many?"

"Eight in the litter." Her voice sounded strained. She wasn't very good at deception. She had better pray the pastor stayed behind her where he couldn't see her face. "These are the last two."

"How old?"

"Over three months now."

He crouched down next to Hannah and patted the pup on its rump. "Which one do you like best?"

She held up a black puppy marked with white on its chest and paws.

"My favorite also," Rachel said, her voice steadier. She stepped down to the ground. "We may keep that one."

"I think she wants the pup for herself, Rach," Caleb said. "She hasn't let go of it."

"Well, that's up to your father, Hannah. It might be hard to watch after both you and a puppy."

Hannah turned hopeful eyes on him. And he sighed. A puppy would be more work.

"Caleb," Reverend Crouse said. "The Women's Circle is meeting in one hour. Get on over to the church and sweep the meeting room before we sit down to eat."

Caleb grimaced, but unloaded the puppy he held. "See you later." He loped across the yard and disappeared into the church's side door.

"You are welcome to join us for supper, Mr. Taylor," said Reverend Crouse.

Stuart would be willing to sit across the table from this man and listen to his preaching if it meant he could be with Rachel a little longer. Of course Hannah would love to stay, but he was afraid he might let something slip out about their trips to the lighthouse. It was obvious Rachel hadn't told the reverend anything.

Stuart took the puppy from his daughter's arms. "No, thanks. I need to get back to the lighthouse. It'll be dark soon."

Shaking his head, Reverend Crouse went inside. A whiff of cooking beans escaped as the door opened and closed.

"He doesn't know." Stuart nodded after the man.

In the lantern light pouring from the kitchen window, Rachel's cheeks flamed scarlet. "I asked him after the picnic. He didn't want me to tutor. He said the people here would fire me. They wouldn't want me teaching their children."

"He's right." He glanced down at the puppy in Hannah's arms. He was stalling, he knew. He didn't want things to change, but he couldn't have Rachel hurt. And after reading Saunders's note, he needed to think about moving on soon. The tutoring would have to stop. "Listen, if you don't have a home for this pup, we'll take him." At his side, Hannah beamed up at him. Perhaps it would help her get through the next few months without Rachel.

"I'll get you a sack for the ride." Rachel disappeared into the house and then came back with an empty flour sack. "He'll be coated with flour dust by the time you get home," she said as she handed it to him.

"No matter." Stuart put the puppy into the sack and tied a knot in the end, then looped it over his saddle horn. "Just for the ride home, little mite. Can't have you falling off and getting hurt." A miniature sneeze erupted from inside the bag.

He lifted Hannah onto Blanco then climbed on behind her. At last he faced Rachel. "Look," he said reluctantly, "I appreciate all you've done with Hannah, but it is time to reconsider this arrangement."

Her gaze flashed to his. "You don't mean that."

He blocked out the hurt in her plea, the ache in his chest. Caring for her only made it more important he do this. He had to take the responsibility to do the right thing. "You shouldn't come anymore, Rachel."

"But—"

He stopped her with a hard stare. "Don't come anymore."

With a slight tilt to his seat he urged Blanco from the yard. Out on the street he couldn't keep himself from looking back once. She stood, a lone black figure silhouetted against the shadow of the house.

Stuart whipped the rope around the bar and pulled it taut, then tied a half hitch to secure the dory in place. The wind had kicked up during the night, and the surf, higher than usual, had pounded against the lean-to, undermining one of the support beams. Days would pass before he could get to town for the supplies to fix it. Besides, he wanted to avoid town.

A bittersweet ache started in the pit of his belly... again. Like a knife already planted there, twisting, always twisting. This was crazy! He had no right to even think of her, let alone want her. How many times had he told himself over the past month that he didn't deserve her?

He spun on his heel and walked down the beach calling for Hannah. He found her searching through the tidal pools, the pup dancing around her heels.

"What have you found now?"

She held up a sand dollar and signed that she was saving it for Rachel.

"Rachel isn't coming anymore, Hannah. You know that."

She signed something more.

"Slow down. I can't read that fast," he said, impatient with her for bringing up the name he was trying so hard to forget. Then, angry at himself for being grouchy, he sat down on a rock to pay closer attention.

She signed again, slower this time.

He dragged his hand through his hair. "No, you didn't do anything wrong. She had to stop the lessons because—" He stopped abruptly. How could he explain things like social rules to a girl who knew nothing of people?

He gazed down the long expanse of beach. How would he stand the silence?

Funny how a man could look strong on the outside, yet on the inside feel so incredibly weary. A deep ache settled in his chest. He had tried not to care. All those he cared for he eventually hurt.

A man takes care of his own. Dorian had ingrained that truth in him from the moment he'd first signed on his ship. He'd believed those words—he still did. Yet he'd failed with Linnea. He couldn't risk failing with Rachel, too.

Hannah climbed on the rock and sat quietly beside him, in tune with the glum wanderings of his mind. He wrapped an arm around her, squeezing her close, and watched the sun start into the sea.

Chapter Fifteen

Stuart dumped a scoop of oats into the feeding bucket and stifled a yawn. He wasn't getting enough sleep. At least not enough good sleep. The minute his eyes closed he had visions of Rachel. Rachel leaning over Hannah as she studied. Rachel walking along the beach as the breeze made her bonnet ribbons dance. Green eyes. Always those green eyes. He gripped the edge of his workbench, letting the rough wood punish his palms. God he missed her. She had worked her way into his life and now his heart. Had it only been ten days since he last saw her? It seemed like an age. Yet there was no way he could see her again. It had to be over.

The sound of horse hooves against packed dirt caught his ear. He strode to the shed's door and stopped. Caleb had pulled Jericho up to the picket fence and stopped the carriage. Hannah bounded down the light-house steps, making a beeline for Rachel. Wide awake now, Stuart walked up and with his body, blocked

Rachel's climb from the carriage. "Turn around now and head back."

Her stormy look held a warning. "I'm going to explain and you are going to listen."

Hannah tugged at his sleeve, a hopeful expression on her upturned face. He wavered. A little. "All right. Five minutes." He reached up and helped Rachel from the carriage.

"Caleb?" Rachel called over her shoulder.

Her brother looped the reins about the brake handle. "I'll watch her. Come here, Hannah." Jumping down, he stepped to the back of the carriage and lifted a crate from the boot.

The lobster trap.

The anger Stuart had felt just a moment before released into the wind with his exhale. They'd come a long way—he and Caleb—since that morning he'd stolen the trap. Caleb waited, and when Stuart nodded his acknowledgment, set the trap down.

Without a word Stuart picked up the crate and took it to the shed. He didn't trust himself with Rachel right now. He wanted to hold her, to shake some sense into her. She should leave immediately.

He knew she had followed him when her shadow blocked the light from the doorway. He turned on her, irritated at her stubbornness, frustrated because to see her had started that ache in his chest he knew wouldn't stop. He strode toward her and pulled her from the door into the shadowed interior of the shed. "What will be your excuse today?"

The shocked look on her face quickly turned to

defiance. "Well, that's a fine hello. I'll think of someth—"

He stopped her words with a kiss, crushing her firm body to him until he could feel the length of her against him. Her hat fell off as he forced her back, her mouth stiff against his lips. It only added to his frustration. He didn't want to hurt her, but she hurt him just by being here. He was tired of playing the saint.

A shooting pain erupted in his foot as she stomped down hard. With a growl he pushed her away, watching her stumble back a step before he grabbed her arm to help her catch her balance.

Her chin went up. "Stop it, Stuart. Don't you dare kiss me in anger." Her voice trembled with suppressed emotion, and her cheeks flushed pink.

He swiped the back of his hand across his lips. "I suppose I deserved that. But dammit, Rachel, you shouldn't be here. People in town are noticing."

"It's none of their business." Her eyes glistened with unshed tears.

He dragged in a brace of air and slowly let it out, willing his heart to stop racing. "You're right about that. But whether you like it or not, your reputation is important. It's important to me. If I'd given any thought to the situation I'd have stopped the tutoring before it started. I wasn't thinking right when I first agreed to it."

She straightened her shoulders. "It wasn't all about Hannah, Stuart, as much as you may think that. I needed someone to take an interest in Caleb. He was running with the wrong group in town. His so-called friends had just set fire to one of the hide houses. They could have torched the whole town. Then at the picnic he lit that firecracker and caused Benjamin to fall. Things were out of hand. I needed help. I explained that when we first agreed to the tutoring."

"Fair enough. We both helped each other. It was a good arrangement. But it stops now." Didn't she realize he had needs? That having her so near did crazy things to him?

She crouched down to pick up her hat from the dirt floor.

"Hannah and I are thinking about moving on, anyway."

Rachel slowed as she stood, her knuckles white on the hat's brim. "You're leaving?"

He hated the plaintive question. She would think it was just one more person walking out on her, but he couldn't tell her the truth. It was better that she didn't learn he was hiding out from a murder and that Hannah wasn't his. He couldn't bear the look in her eyes if she ever discovered that. "Something's come up. And with the tutoring finished, now is a good time."

"Oh." Slowly she turned toward the door.

"I'd like to say I'm sorry about the kiss, but I'm not." He wanted much more than to kiss her. Much more.

She wouldn't look at him. "I…I'd like to spend some time with Hannah, then. And Caleb hoped to go fishing with you one more time."

He saw through her to the hurt she felt inside. He wanted to kiss it away. Wanted to hold her. He stepped forward. "Rach…" And then thought better of it. "All right. I'll take him fishing. Then we'll say our goodbyes."

Fishing turned out to be nonproductive in spite of the old tale that fish bite best before a storm. The clouds overhead had thickened into a dark-gray mass and the wind had kicked up to a mild gale that had the portent to get much worse.

Stuart started to reel in his line. "This weather is turning bad. We'd better give this up for today."

Caleb pointed out to sea. "Look at that. What are they doing out in this?"

Stuart squinted. A white sail. "I don't know. Not too smart, though. It's beyond choppy."

He stood, and the first large drops of rain splattered against his face. He made his way across the rock, finding it slippery as the rain started pelting down.

Suddenly Caleb yelled, "The boat has gone over!"

Stuart whirled around and spotted the white over-turned hull of the boat, the keel listing in the growing swells. Three men clung to the boat.

"We'll need the dory," Stuart said.

They dropped their fishing gear and raced toward the lean-to. On the sand the boat was awkward and heavy. Stuart was glad to have Caleb's help maneuvering it around and into the water. By the time they made it through the waves, they were both soaked to the skin.

The wind whipped rain into their faces while they rowed out to sea. The sky had darkened to iron-metal gray, making it difficult to see the vessel between the swells. Determination filled Caleb's features, and he matched Stuart's rowing, stroke for stroke. A flash of pride surged through Stuart. The past two months had wrought a definite change in the boy.

Stuart pulled hard at the oars, straining against the battering waves. "Bear to port."

Caleb raised his brows.

"Left! Head left!"

They were thirty feet from the overturned vessel when one of the men pushed himself off and swam madly for them.

"No!" Stuart shouted. Visions of Linnea sinking in the water choked his mind. "Hang on! We'll get closer!" He hurled a coil of rope toward the struggling man. It unwound in the fierce wind and fell short of its goal.

"Samuel!" Caleb yelled.

The young man's blond head disappeared once beneath a swell, then resurfaced, panic slashed across his face.

"I'll get him," Caleb yelled and started to place his oars in the bed of the boat.

"No!" Stuart shouted. "He's tangled in the kelp. Bring the dory alongside."

Five hard strokes and they came abreast of Samuel. Fear was etched deep into the sharp angles of his face. He flailed his arms, trying to move closer to the boat. Caleb leaned over the dory's side, his stomach pressed against the hard ridge of wood, and stretched out his hands.

Samuel clamped on with a death grip.

"Hang on!" Caleb ground out through clenched teeth, pulling against the heavier weight. He slid toward the water. Stuart sprang forward and anchored Caleb's feet. For an instant Sam furrowed through a rising swell, dragging a heavy line of kelp around his legs. Then he lost his grip and slipped under the surface.

Stuart yanked Caleb back into the boat, relieved he hadn't followed Sam into the water. He searched for a trace of the boy. A field of amber kelp twisted just beneath surface, thick and tangled.

"We gotta do something!" Caleb cried. Desperation filled his face. He looked wildly about the floor of the dory. Suddenly he pulled his knife from his pocket.

Stuart lunged forward. "No! Caleb!"

But Caleb dove into the frigid water and Stuart's fingers closed on empty air.

Stuart looked at the men hanging from the sailboat hull and knew his eyes mirrored the dread that filled theirs. If he jumped in after Caleb like his gut instinct told him to do, those men would pay with their lives if he didn't return. So he stayed where he was, gripping the edge of the dory, ready to drag Caleb aboard the second he surfaced.

A full minute passed with no sign of either boy. Then Sam broke the water's surface and dragged in a lungful of air. Stuart lunged toward him, grabbed his shirt and then hoisted under his arms while the boy inched his leg over the side of the dory and fell into the boat, coughing and spitting out saltwater.

Seconds later Caleb surfaced.

"Thank God!" Stuart breathed and tugged the boy into the boat.

Caleb shivered violently.

Stuart grabbed Caleb by the collar and shook him. "You're lucky you didn't just go to meet your Maker. Don't you ever pull a stunt like that again!" He locked his arm about Caleb's neck and hugged him tight.

The sailboat floated thirty feet away now. Swells rose in a contrary rhythm between the two crafts, propelling them apart. At one point the gap between the two boats closed enough that Caleb, with a loud grunt, heaved the rope. One man caught the end but there was no place for him to tie it to the boat. He nodded to his companion. "You go, John."

The heavy man clung to the keel of the sailboat and refused to budge.

"Let go," Stuart yelled. "Make your way over."

"I can't! Me arms are bloody numb. I'll sink like a stone if I let go."

Stuart cupped his hands about his mouth. "You don't have a choice. You have to do it."

"I can't, I tell you. There's got to be another way."

Caleb leaned toward Stuart, a question in his eyes. "I could jump in again."

"No!" Stuart roared. "Help me on the rope. We'll get closer."

Together they pulled, straining against the swells, hand over hand, until the dory came alongside the sailboat. Stuart's fingers were nerveless from the cold. How had the men managed to hang on for so long?

John floundered like a big fish, struggling to climb into the dory. Stuart and Caleb grabbed each of his arms and heaved up. With a final, awkward kick, John landed in the bottom of the boat.

"You next, Russ!" Sam yelled through chattering teeth.

Russ gripped the rope with both hands and let Caleb and Stuart pull him across the water and into the dory.

The three sailors lay sprawled across the floor of the boat, shivering and wet, but alive.

Stuart took up his oars and with Caleb's help turned the dory toward the beach. Soon the boat surged ahead and he had the chance to consider his "catch." Russ appeared to be in his fifties and John somewhat younger, perhaps thirty-five. Sam, the youngest, stared at Caleb with a closed expression. By the cut of his clothes, Stuart pegged him for a "Sunday" fisherman.

A thought blindsided him. They were from La Playa—at least Sam was—which meant they knew Rachel. A sinking sensation filled him and he searched for another choice rather than to take them to the lighthouse. His gaze lighted on John—wet, cold, and exhausted—and he had his answer. There *was* no better choice.

Rachel pulled the cotton curtain aside and peered through the rain-streaked window. Something was wrong—terribly wrong. Otherwise Stuart and Caleb would have been back rather than out in this foul weather. She brushed her fingertips over her bruised lips, remembering the embrace. Remembering how her body had wanted to respond, although she refused to give in. Never had she seen Stuart so angry.

And he was leaving.

She turned and paced the length of the small kitchen. Where could he be? Why hadn't he returned by now? She checked the coffeepot for the umpteenth time to make sure the coffee hadn't boiled away, just as Hannah dashed from the kitchen table to the door. But instead of shutting the door after looking outside, she swung it wide with a bang.

Rachel followed her to the door to find not only Caleb and Stuart, but three other men soaked to the skin.

"Their boat capsized just off the rock," Stuart said.

He had a scrape along his right cheek, red and raw, but not bleeding. She glanced quickly over Caleb. Although he was wet and shivering, otherwise he looked unharmed. "Is everyone all right?"

A heavy, bearded man stepped forward and nodded. "Thanks to Caleb and Mr. Taylor, miss. Just soaked through to the bones."

She recognized the boy at the rear of the group. "Samuel?"

He nodded. "It's me under all this water."

"Your family will be relieved to know you're well."

Stuart caught her attention. "Would you make coffee while I find towels and blankets?"

"Of course. Please, all of you come in by the fire and dry off." She grabbed a chair from the kitchen and carried it into the parlor to set it close before the small brick fireplace. She'd kept the fire going, finding it cheery on this stormy afternoon, but now she tossed on extra coal for added warmth.

When she turned and dusted off her hands, she caught the men watching her. She could feel the precise moment their looks turned to speculation about why she was here. Warmth flooded her cheeks and she fled to the kitchen, wanting to evaporate on the spot. Since disappearing into the cracks in the limestone wall wasn't an option, she busied herself making strong coffee and trying to erase the embarrassment from her mind.

Upstairs, Stuart called for Hannah to gather towels and blankets. Before a cricket would have had time to warm up his legs, Hannah returned, loaded down with comforters, and shyly passed them out to the shivering group.

When Stuart didn't return immediately, Rachel wondered what he was doing, but then through the window she saw the lamp's beam of light sweep across the low cloud cover. The sight did little to comfort her jumpy nerves. It was getting dark. She should be on her way home.

She didn't want to go back into the parlor and face the questioning stares of the men. She wanted to slip out with Caleb and pretend none of this had happened. But the coffee was ready, they were cold, and hiding in the kitchen wasn't helping anybody. She stepped over to the stove and filled each mug. Footsteps sounded on the circular stairs and at their sound relief grew in her— relief that she wouldn't have to face the men alone. She placed the mugs on a tray and looked up as Stuart appeared.

He had changed from his wet clothes into dry pants and was fastening the last button on his shirt when he stopped at the bottom of the stairs. "You know your way around this kitchen like it was yours."

"Unfortunately, I believe the men noticed that too. Stuart—what should we tell them?"

He rubbed his forehead, his eyes clouding with concern. "Nothing. We'll say nothing." He sighed. "We didn't count on this. Come on. We'll go in together."

The men sat in front of the fireplace rubbing their hands before the heat. Each murmured thanks and told her his name when he took his mug of steaming coffee but still she felt the questions behind their politeness. They sipped the coffee and soon looked more revived from their ordeal.

"So—" Stuart said, sitting Hannah on his knee. "How did it happen?"

John shifted in his seat. "Samuel, you might as well tell it. I expect he'll be makin' a report."

Stuart nodded, but Sam didn't say anything.

"It's a bit embarrassin' y' see," John explained. "We were fishing the kelp beds. Got an early start this mornin'. Expected the weather to clear off like it usually does by ten or so. The bloody storm took us by surprise." He glanced at Rachel. "Excuse my language, miss."

Sam looked up from his place on the floor. "We did catch two good-size yellowtail. Guess that don't matter now. We figured we had time to catch one more fish. Then the wind came up and we laughed about having a race to the harbor. We hoisted the sail and right away a gust slammed into the sheet and tipped the boat way over. Russ lost his balance and fell into me and I grabbed on to John. The next thing I knew we all were in the water and the boat was upside down."

John slapped his knee. "Young Sam here wanted to swim for shore! Only thing that stopped him was he knew the rest of us couldn't make it. At least not me. My whole body was numb."

"You were right to stay with the boat," Stuart said.

"How'd you find us?"

"We were fishing off the large rock, just getting ready to leave when Caleb spotted you."

Samuel met Caleb's gaze. "Thanks for jumping in after me. Guess what I did was pretty dumb."

The men glanced at each other.

"After all," Sam continued, "all I ever done since you moved here was get you in trouble."

Caleb shrugged. "I've always been a pretty good swimmer."

Rachel gasped, looking from one boy to the next. "You didn't go in, Caleb! Tell me you didn't!"

"I'm all right, Rach."

His words did not reassure her. "How would I live with myself? Never, never do such a thing again!"

"He won't have another chance." Finality filled Stuart's voice. He slid Hannah from his knee. "When you get to town," he said to Caleb, "let Sam's folks know about the accident. Have them send a wagon back."

"That sounds fine," John said. "My brother will want to reward you, anyway."

Rachel started. It was embarrassing enough these men knew she was here. But the whole town—what if everyone found out? How could she face them? She met Stuart's gaze and knew he was thinking the same thoughts.

"No reward," he said quickly.

"But you're a hero! Both of you!" Samuel sputtered.

"I was doing my job."

John shrugged his shoulders. "Have it your way, then. What about you Caleb? We'd still be out there if it weren't for you. You're the one who spotted us and dove in after Sam."

All eyes turned to Caleb. His face turned pink in the firelight as he basked in John's praise, but he shook his head. "No reward."

Rachel could have kissed him.

"All right. I doubt you'll ever see us out there for a second chance."

Murmurs of agreement filled the room.

"Is there any hope of saving the sailboat?" Samuel asked.

Stuart shook his head. "I'll keep an eye out for it, but most likely it will be smashed on the rocks by morning."

Rachel glanced out the window. Rain pelted steadily against the glass and the sky was a deep pewter color. The ride home would be a slow, wet one. She stood and gathered the mugs. "I'll just be a minute."

She hurried from the room, feeling their stares marking her back. In the kitchen, she set the cups into the large wash pan on the stove, then poured steaming water from the kettle over the few dishes. She was suddenly acutely aware she could never return here, never work with Hannah again, never see Stuart again. Her eyes stung.

"Not much light left," Stuart said from the doorway, "but enough to get you home if you leave the dishes and start now." Hannah stood at his side, clinging to his arm.

Her hands stilled in the wash water. "It's over, isn't it?"

He dragged a hand through his hair. "You're a big

girl, Rachel. I think you had an idea when you started coming here that a day like today was inevitable. I don't want you in any more trouble on my account."

When had seeing him become as important to her as breathing?

She dried her hands and held open her arms to Hannah. Crouching down, she hugged the girl tightly. Tears blurred her vision, but she kept her smile in place. "You must keep practicing your letters so you can write to me."

Hannah nodded.

"Check on Sarah," Stuart said quietly, nodding his head toward the stairs. "I'll be up soon."

After Hannah left, Rachel turned back to Stuart. "The other night at my house, you were right to tell me not to come. I understood the consequences. But Stuart, given the chance, I'd do it all again. I have no regrets."

He placed his hands firmly on her shoulders. The heat from his palms burned into her skin, familiar now, reassuring. "We haven't done anything wrong, Rachel. Don't let them tell you that you have."

She looked into his blue eyes. How could she never come back? Never see him again? Her chest ached at the thought. With trembling fingers, she brushed the familiar wisp of hair off his brow, and then just as slowly traced the bruise forming around the gash on his cheek. *So many scars.*

His gaze locked on hers. "Rachel…don't."

A shiver raced through her. He pulled her against his chest and she breathed in the scent of rain on his skin. His heartbeat pounded in her ear, and she thought he must have stopped breathing because surely she had.

"I gave you fair warning," he murmured. With strong fingers he tilted her head back and slowly lowered his mouth to hers. Tenderly he deepened the kiss until he seemed to draw out her very soul. If not for holding him about his neck, she'd have fallen.

"Rachel," he whispered, his warm breath caressing her ear. "I'm sorry if I've hurt you."

Beneath her hands, the muscles in his shoulders rippled. He kissed her once more, softly this time. This kiss said goodbye. Slowly he pulled away.

"Stuart, I—"

He pressed his fingertips to her mouth. "Don't. Just go."

She stood there, shaken, while he spun around and headed for the stairs. With a trembling hand she brushed her fingertips across her lips. "I'm not sorry. Not for any of it," she whispered. He paused at her words but did not look back, then continued up the stairs two at a time.

She stepped outside, barely noticing the stinging wind on her cheeks, and closed the door behind her.

Chapter Sixteen

The final notes of "God of Our Fathers" rang out over the small congregation. Rachel sighed with relief. Only the closing hymn to get through while everyone filed out of the church.

She glanced up from the piano and met Terrance's gaze in the third pew. Her stomach rolled into a knot. Again. Throughout the service he'd watched her, a suspicious stare on his face. He couldn't know about her part in the boat rescue, could he? Her cheeks heated with the thought. She looked out over the congregation. Sam and his family were conspicuously absent.

Reverend Crouse said the benediction, and she stretched out her fingers and forced herself to begin the final hymn. When the last person had left the building to join those visiting on the street, Terrance strode toward her.

"A little rusty today," he said, raising one eyebrow. "Two mistakes."

She closed the hymnal with a thud. "I'd better practice this week."

"Thought you were out at the Hummels' on Friday." His eyes sharpened on her hers. "I rode out there to deliver their new water pump. Didn't see you."

A moment of panic seized her. She wouldn't lie, but what could she say? "The weather turned so ugly that I decided to return early."

He watched her face closely. Her heart pounding, she put the hymnal back on the small music shelf.

"Are you still coming for dinner today?"

She had completely forgotten their plans!

Terrance's smile appeared strained. "You know, your face is transparent at times. I'll be by for you at one o'clock. Don't forget."

When he left, Rachel slumped on the bench and stared at the piano keys. Terrance had been toying with her. He knew something.

By Wednesday Rachel felt a little calmer. It appeared no one was wise to her recent excursions and life could go on as though her time with Stuart and Hannah hadn't existed. The thought was both comforting and disturbing. In her heart she'd never forget it.

How could something that felt so right be so wrong?

She cleaned up the remnants of breakfast from the table and dumped the scraps into a bowl for Settie. Today would be her day for getting on with her life. After school, her first stop would be the mercantile to mail her application for the teacher's certification test.

Someone banged on the front door. Before she could

reach it, Terrance burst in, his face twisted with anger. In one hand he held the keys to his store and in the other, the *San Diego Herald*.

"Rachel!" Fury filled his voice when he caught sight of her.

Apprehension stilled her. "What is it?"

"That's what I'd like to know. I was just opening the store when I saw this." He shook the newspaper. "What were you and Caleb doing at the lighthouse?"

"Let me see, Terrance," she said, striving to remain calm.

He shoved the newspaper at her. A front-page story lauding Stuart and Caleb's heroic rescue paraded before her eyes.

"Oh, no," she murmured and sank to a chair. The newspaper! This was much worse than she could have imagined. Now the entire town would know.

"What is going on?" Terrance demanded.

Certain phrases stood out more sharply than others. Phrases such as: "The coffee served by Miss Rachel Houston did much to revive the spirits of the soggy fishermen before they took their leave." She leaned over and covered her face with her hands.

Terrance finally sat in the chair opposite her. "Don't even think about coming up with a lie."

"Terrance—"

His usually pale complexion had turned a mottled pink. "I don't know what kind of game you are playing but I won't have it played on me! You've been out to that lighthouse more than just once. That girl is learning her letters and hand signals. Admit it! All these weeks you've been spending time with that dumb girl and her father."

The attack on Hannah helped Rachel stiffen her spine. "She is not dumb!"

Terrance jabbed at the paper. "What were you doing out there? He's the same man who shot at Enrique! You know he's not stable."

"They were just warning shots. And Enrique deserved a scare. He stole from Mr. Taylor's lobster traps, as a regular occurrence, I might add."

Terrance paced back and forth. "It's different when you see him in town. He wouldn't dare raise a hand to you here, but out there he is on his own land. You would have no protection from him."

"He's not dangerous. You are blowing this all out of proportion, Terrance."

"Do you admit you've been out there more than once?"

"You're doing an excellent job of putting two and two together." Anger built inside her. She didn't deserve his outrage. He didn't have any say over her. "I have my reasons for doing what I did and they are good ones. You don't own me."

Terrance stepped back at her words. "Does Reverend Crouse know?" he asked.

"No. Not yet at least. Not until he reads this." She slapped the newspaper down on the tea wagon between them. "Terrance, all I've done is help Hannah. Is that such a terrible thing?"

"How long has this been going on, Rachel?"

She sighed, noticing how he'd ignored her question. "Since the picnic."

"The picnic! That was over three months ago!"

"I felt I—the church—owed the man something after he saved Benjamin."

"What else has he demanded in payment?"

"Nothing!" Rachel cried, shocked at what he suggested. "And he didn't demand the tutoring. All he cares about is his daughter and her happiness. Trust me on this, Terrance."

"Trust you! How? Why?"

"I've done nothing wrong."

He looked at her down his long nose. "Prove it, then. Prove to me he hasn't taught you a thing or two while you've been teaching his child."

He grabbed her arms and pulled her toward him. She struggled, suddenly frightened of this new Terrance.

He stared hard at her a moment and then shoved her away. "I guess you haven't learned much."

She trembled. "You need to leave, Terrance. I'll see you after you've calmed down."

"If I thought he had touched you, I would…" He sighed and didn't continue.

But he left more than enough room for her to worry. The way he said the words scared her—so quietly, so very calmly.

"I know we weren't officially courting, Rachel, but I thought we had an understanding."

She tried to gather her thoughts. "There have been no words of commitment between you and me. Just friendship. Until now."

He snorted. "My sister was right. I put you on a

pedestal. The daughter of a gold panner. What a fool."
He squared his shoulders. "There will be talk at the
township meeting tomorrow night. Are you still planning to take the teacher's examination?"

"Yes, of course."

"The school board members may not want you
teaching their children."

Stunned, she stuttered, "No…they wouldn't go that
far." Would they?

"This affects everything." He waved the newspaper in
the air. "I've lived here all my life. I know these people."

"Terrance. Caleb was with me."

"Every time?"

She nodded. "Yes."

"I'll mention that in my report. I don't know that it
will help much."

"Thank you." Her intentions had only been for good.
How had they become so distorted?

"Rachel Houston!" The kitchen door slammed shut.
Reverend Crouse stomped down the hall and into the
parlor, followed quickly by his wife. He ignored
Terrance and slapped another copy of the newspaper
into her lap. "Explain yourself!"

"I…uh…"

"Have you been at the lighthouse?"

She nodded, miserable. "I've been tutoring Hannah."

The reverend suddenly noticed Terrance. "I hope you
realize this has been without my knowledge, Mr. Morley."

Terrance nodded. "We've discussed it. The article
disrupted an otherwise peaceful morning."

Terrance looked at her as though she were a misguided child. "I believe Rachel when she says that nothing happened, but there are people that won't."

Emma Crouse nodded. "Mabel and Phyllis Olsen came to see me this morning. They wanted answers. This is only the beginning." She bustled over to sit next to Rachel on the settee. "Are you all right, dear? Has he done anything to hurt you?"

Rachel shook her head. "No. He has acted the gentleman on each occasion." She refused to tell them about the one time when he kissed her in anger.

"Well, then it will all work out. You'll see." Emma hugged her firmly.

Reverend Crouse picked up his copy of the paper. "You'll have to bear the consequences of your actions. They may not be pleasant."

"I wasn't naive about my choice in this. If it causes any repercussions on your ministry—well, that I hadn't counted on."

He sighed and patted her hand awkwardly. "It won't matter there. Emma and I have had to handle many situations over the years."

Terrance squared his shoulders. "It's earlier than we anticipated, but perhaps this would be the opportune time to announce our engagement. A solid front would help ward off the gossips."

Startled, Rachel looked up at Terrance. "You're serious," she said, amazed at the turn in conversation.

He nodded.

"But why?" After seeing what lay beneath his surface, she was sure he wasn't for her. Besides, her heart was already taken, whether Stuart wanted it or not.

The reverend looked just as surprised as she felt, but recovered quickly, a smile growing on his face. "Yes. Yes! Splendid idea."

"No." She stood, and repeated firmly, "No."

Terrance frowned. "You've made a mess of things, Rachel. It's up to you to fix them. Besides, marrying me will take the pressure off. You can help in the mercantile and you won't need to worry about teaching anymore. You won't even have to bother with the examination."

Terrance took her hands in his, his voice smooth and gentle—so gentle she could almost forget the bruising pressure of his fingers on her shoulders just moments before. "This is where we were heading—you and I. We'll just shorten the usual waiting time. People won't dare talk about my fiancée if they want to do business with me."

"I…I'm not sure I…"

"Trust me in this. You'll find it's the sensible thing to do. You've let your heart rule, rather than your head. Unfortunately, that is a hazard of being a woman."

She stiffened.

"Don't misunderstand me," he said quickly. "Your soft heart will be an asset when dealing with me and with the children we'll have one day. I'll balance it as the one expected to discipline and keep you all in line."

A sickening sensation built in her stomach. He was serious! After all she'd been through with her father—living in a tent with the dust and the flies, trying to make dinner out of hard tack and gruel, following him from stream to stream in search of gold—she wasn't about to give up her independence over something like this, no matter what happened to her reputation. She pulled her hands from his. "This is a noble gesture, Terrance, but the truth is…I don't love you."

Chapter Seventeen

"I don't care what you say," Amanda Furst declared and hung the last crocheted ornament on the pine tree. "A Christmas without snow is not Christmas at all."

Amanda, Elizabeth and Rachel were putting the finishing touches on the decorations for the community party that evening. The meeting room in the Mexican Custom House was just the right size for the gathering. They had pushed the chairs to the walls to make room for dancing to the mariachi band and hung large bows on each of the wall sconces to perk up the plain room. The pine tree filled one corner and the podium another.

From her perch on the ladder, Elizabeth fastened a sprig of mistletoe to the front doorway and exchanged a smile with Amanda. Rachel wondered at their sudden friendship. Elizabeth had never been one to put up with Amanda before, but ever since the newspaper article came out three weeks ago, they'd begun doing things together…and excluding Rachel. They only helped with the party preparations today because they had promised weeks ago.

Rachel steadied the ladder as Elizabeth climbed down, and then they moved it to the center of the room to hang the piñata, a festively painted pottery jar filled with candy and dried fruit.

"Are the games ready?" Elizabeth asked after securing the rope that would be used to raise and lower the piñata. It was the first question she'd directed at Rachel all afternoon.

Rachel nodded.

"Then I guess we are done," she said, wiping her hands on her apron. "I need to get back to help at the store."

Amanda shrugged into her cloak and flipped her blond hair over her fox fur collar. "Sorry I can't stay and help clean up the mess. I'll walk over with you, Liz."

Rachel watched them go, hurt by their uncharacteristic coolness, then began picking up the trail of colored ribbons and cut paper snowflakes. She adjusted the poinsettia arrangement on the table for the fourth time, wishing the party tonight was already over. She didn't want to face the stares and whispered speculations, but Reverend and Emma Crouse depended on her help. Emma had told her she must act as if everything was fine, that she'd done nothing wrong. The same way she'd been acting for the past three weeks. When were people going to recognize the truth for what it was and let things get back to normal?

The cleanup didn't take long, and soon Rachel left, walking to the parsonage while the sun set and sent its last splash of orange-pink rays spreading across the harbor.

That evening she dressed carefully—a cream-colored, full-skirted dress with a deep-blue sash. She had sown tiny seed pearls in two rows along the modest neckline. It had been tedious work, but she found that it soothed her. Since she was no longer tutoring, she'd had time to take out Caleb's pants at the cuffs and even help Emma with some of her mending. Bolstering her courage to face those at the party, she threw her cloak over her shoulders and headed out the door.

Rachel took a place next to Emma and helped serve the cider punch as people arrived. Terrance showed up with Amanda on his arm and Elizabeth at his side. They stood across the room as the children recited passages from the Book of Matthew. Benjamin played the angel bearing tidings of great joy. When the door opened and a gust of damp air blew through the room, he faltered in his speaking lines. A stranger strode in, noticed the Christmas play in progress and pulled back against the wall to watch.

After the short play Reverend Crouse addressed the group and then everyone sang a round of their favorite carols while Rachel accompanied on the piano. She tried to steel herself against the stares of several people, telling herself it was curiosity on their part—not true ill thoughts about her.

Caleb started off the games. He blindfolded little Maria and spun her around, then pointed her toward the piñata, handing her the end of a sawed-off broomstick.

Everyone stepped back. Maria swung while Terrance pulled on the rope, raising and lowering the pottery jar.

Nine children took their turns before the tenth one broke the jar. Squeals of delight filled the air as candies and fruit rained down upon them. The children scattered over the floor, grabbing handfuls of sweets. Hannah would have fun with this game. The sudden onset of tears made Rachel squeeze her eyes shut. Oh, would she ever get over this?

The evening wore on and everyone had their fill of cider and fruitcake and candies. For the last game before the dancing, Rachel had fashioned a large spider out of wire and hung it from the ceiling. Ribbons of every color crisscrossed and wound about the room, acting as the spider's web.

She lined up the children and handed each of them a piece of ribbon. "Your Christmas present is at the end of the ribbon that matches your swatch."

She found herself grinning while the children followed the ribbons down from the spider and worked through the maze of colors to find their presents. It was all such a tangled mess of fun for the little ones. Before long, small hands clutched paper dolls, whirligigs and Jacob's ladders. She looked up to see Terrance staring at her from across the room.

Behind her, Amanda whispered loudly, "You obviously have been leading Terrance on. You haven't been honest with him. He still thinks there is a chance between you two. Someone should set him straight."

Her attack hurt and Rachel turned to face her. "You, for instance?" When Amanda didn't say anything, she added, "I bet you are happy to have Samuel back in one piece."

Amanda looked at her flatly. "Yes. Yes, I am. Too bad it made things more difficult for you." At her side, Elizabeth said nothing before turning away with Amanda.

Rachel clenched her hands at her side. Why had she ever considered Amanda her friend? Her words hurt, but even more was the way others had followed her lead. Amanda was the prettiest, richest girl on the peninsula. If she led a vendetta against Rachel, Rachel would have a difficult time keeping her teaching job at the school.

Emma Crouse stepped up. "Give them time, dear. They'll see."

Rachel drew in a shaky breath. "They're so spiteful."

"Yes. They are."

She sighed and forced a small smile as Pastor Crouse joined them and then suddenly kissed his wife on her cheek.

"You are in a dangerous area, dear, standing under that weed. I may have to steal another kiss."

Emma Crouse looked up to find the mistletoe above her. A blush painted her crinkled cheeks. "Stanley! Behave!"

Rachel relaxed slightly. She'd made it through the worst of the evening. Only a little longer and she could slip away gracefully.

People began to cluster in the center of the room as the four men in the mariachi band started warming up. A stranger, a short man with brown hair and spectacles, started toward them.

"Pastor Crouse?"

"Yes," the reverend said, turning. "What can I do for you?"

"Name is Pittman. Sorry to interrupt the festivities. My timing is not always the best."

"What can I do for you, Mr. Pittman?"

"I was looking for the owner of the mercantile. It was closed up tight when I went by just now."

"Mr. Morley?"

"Yes. That's right. Is he here?"

Reverend Crouse called across the room to Caleb. "Run outside and get Terrance for me. He's talking with Luis Rose and Thomas Whaley."

Caleb gave a quick nod and hurried out the door.

"I'm interested in information concerning Matthew and Hannah Taylor. Do you know of them?"

Rachel's heart skipped a beat.

"Are you a friend of the Taylors'?" the reverend asked.

"Oh, no. I'm here on official business."

She stepped forward. "There is no Matthew Taylor."

The man turned his attention to her for the first time, and a chill went up her back. "Perhaps he goes by Stuart, then. They are one and the same."

Terrance appeared at her side. "I'm Terrance Morley. You wanted to speak with me?" His eyes seemed brighter than normal as he glanced from Mr. Pittman to Rachel.

"He's asking after the Taylors," she said.

Mr. Pittman unfolded a newspaper he had tucked under his arm and pointed to the rescue article. "I believe you sent this to me, Mr. Morley?" At Terrance's brief nod, he continued, "I'm Detective Pittman. Matthew Taylor stole property from Lansing Enterprises three years ago. There is a reward out for information on his whereabouts."

Stunned, Rachel could only exclaim, "No…there must be some mistake!"

"Oh, I'm quite sure I have the facts straight. Mr. Lansing has hired me to find Taylor and arrest him."

Then the rumors had been right? Stuart had been a criminal all along? She looked at Caleb's face and saw that his doubt mirrored her own. Had they both been naive in trusting the man? A weight settled in the pit of her stomach. "He wouldn't do anything illegal. He's not like that."

Terrance made a sound of disgust. "Rachel—you don't know the man. It's quite odd Taylor showed up here just after this property was stolen."

"Oh there's more to it than stolen property," Mr. Pittman said. "Much more. Taylor is also wanted for kidnapping and murder."

The room grew quiet as everyone turned their attention on Detective Pittman and Rachel.

"What?" Her voice trembled. "That can't be true. I won't believe it."

"Well, that's convenient for Taylor," Terrance said snidely.

It had to be a mistake. Stuart had said his wife drowned. She rubbed her temple. She had to think, had to reason it all out. How had Terrance known to contact this detective? "Who is this Lansing?"

"You should know," Terrance said. "Does Lansing Shipping mean anything to you?"

Her eyes widened. The mercantile frequently got cargo with that imprint on the crates.

Caleb snorted. "And here I thought Taylor was so perfect. Even took that lobster trap back to him. He shouldn't be pointing any fingers!"

Caleb! Don't think so of him. Not after all he has done for you. But Rachel couldn't voice her thoughts. She didn't know who to believe.

"Where could I find him now?" Mr. Pittman asked, looking from Terrance to Rachel.

She took a step backward, shaking her head. She wouldn't tell. She wouldn't be the one to hurt Stuart or Hannah.

"He lives at the lighthouse, about six miles from here," Terrance interjected smoothly. He sighed when he saw her frown. "Rachel, Mr. Pittman here could ask any number of people in town and would get the same response. It's silly to keep it from him."

"Hmm. Rather dark to head out now. And I want to alert the sheriff before confronting the man." Mr. Pittman removed his glasses and wiped the lens with his handkerchief, looking down his nose at those assembled. "I'll wait until morning and get a fresh start. The hotel here appears to have rooms available."

"I'll walk with you, just give me one moment." Terrance took Rachel aside. "Are you going to be all right?"

No, she wanted to scream. *I'll never be all right again.* She tried to ignore Detective Pittman's penetrating stare, and focused on Terrance's face. "How did you learn he was wanted?"

"The last shipment from Lansing held a flyer that asked for information on him. I simply sent the news article."

Any small hope she might have had inside deflated with his words. That article again. She'd give anything to turn back the clock and relive that day differently—except that if she and Caleb had not gone out to the lighthouse, Sam and his friends would surely have drowned.

Terrance placed his hands on her shoulders, forcing her to look up at him. "It had to happen sooner or later. Aren't you glad you are no longer involved with that family? The scandal now will be much worse."

"It's Hannah I'm worried about." But that was a lie. She was worried about Stuart too. "How could you let this happen, Terrance? How could you send for this detective?"

"I could because I care about you. It is too bad Taylor will drag his daughter down with him—if she even is his daughter. But I won't have him dragging you down too. Given time you'll realize I'm right."

Rachel couldn't stay here any longer and listen. She glanced about at the couples pairing off for the dancing and noticed Amanda watching her closely. The room started to swirl as the band began a lively tune. She didn't know if it was the dancers moving or whether it was the sudden wave of dizziness that overcame her, but everything began closing in on her.

She shook loose from Terrance's grip and grabbed her cloak from its peg near the door. "It's late." She looked once more at the paper-strewn room and then at Reverend Crouse. "I'm sorry. I just cannot stay. I…I'll clean up tomorrow."

The reverend frowned. "You are not to go out to that lighthouse," he said, the warning clear in his voice.

Her head pounded with thoughts of Stuart and murder and drowning, and still she knew that the lighthouse was the only place she wanted to be. "Of course not."

"I have your word you'll go straight home?" His eyes bored into hers and she hesitated a moment too long. "Rachel. It's not safe. There are coyotes about. Besides, Taylor could use you as a hostage."

She turned her full attention on him. "How would I see? There's no moon."

"Good. Then Caleb and I will pack up. We'll see you at the house."

She threw her cloak about her shoulders and left, passing through the stares and curious looks of the rest of the townspeople who stood on the fringes of the dance floor.

Her thoughts were in chaos as she hurried the short distance down the dirt street. Something had to be done! Not for a moment was she worried about Stuart using her as a hostage. Reverend Crouse's warnings fell on deaf ears. But to go to Stuart, to go to the lighthouse now would seal her fate. She would be stripped of her teaching position for sure. And she and Caleb would have to move.

She had just turned the doorknob on the parsonage when her toe stubbed against something. The plain brown-paper-wrapped object was slightly larger than Reverend Crouse's Bible. She picked it up, surprised at its heaviness.

Large uneven letters sprawled across the top of the package spelled out Merry Christmas. A tingling sensation started deep within her. She recognized the writing. Hannah. She tore away the paper, revealing a beautiful cherrywood box.

Quickly, she glanced about the yard and street, hoping to see Stuart. There was no sign of anyone. She stepped into the parsonage and lit the gas lamp on the tea trolley, and then sat down on the brocade chair, stroking the smooth wood and running her fingers over the simple design of the box. She unhinged the brass latch and opened the lid.

Inside, a handful of sea shells lined the bottom, along with two large sand dollars and a shiny new pocket knife. Tucked in a corner sat the whale Stuart had carved. Her breath hitched, her emotions spinning. An envelope with her name printed in achingly familiar childlike letters rested among the treasures. Her hands shook as she reached for it. She tore the wax seal and removed a note written in a man's strong script.

Oh, Stuart. Her heart squeezed in her chest.

"Better than fish, right?" it said.

She smiled. He had remembered she didn't like fish. The words blurred as tears filled her eyes.

"The pocket knife is for Caleb. Warn him that it's sharper than the one he 'borrowed.'"

Another smile.

This is a small "thanks" to you and Caleb. Hannah learns new words every day and tugs at my arm constantly so that I will watch her and learn them, too. The shells are from her for Caleb. She wants you to have the sand dollars.

I started making this box after one of your first visits to the lighthouse. Hannah said you once told her you never had your own treasure box. Fill it full, Rachel.
Stuart

She crushed the note to her breast, drawing in an unsteady breath. Closing her eyes, a mental image of him swam before her, the strong angle of his chin, the crystal blue of his eyes. How she missed him—his strength, his teasing, even his stubbornness. He once told her he didn't believe in saving things, yet he had made this for her.

She stroked the smooth edge of the wood, running her fingers from one corner to the other, caressing the grain and thinking all the while of Stuart's strong hands sanding each side. She reached inside for Hannah's small collection of sand dollars and shells, picking them up in turn, knowing Hannah had chosen each one carefully.

He had to be warned. That's all there was to it. She wasn't afraid of him or the dark. And the coyotes were fat off the never-ending supply of rabbits. They wouldn't bother her. Rising, she carried the box upstairs to her room and placed it inside her bureau drawer.

In the kitchen she left a note for the Crouses:

"Don't worry about me. I'm all right. I had to do this."

She fastened the toggles on her cloak at her neck and hurried out to the carriage house to saddle Jericho.

Chapter Eighteen

Stuart leaned over the bed and checked Hannah's forehead. Thank God, no fever. Her eyelids closed and he snuggled the blankets around her. "Sweet dreams, short stuff. You'll feel better tomorrow." He ruffled her hair, then headed up the curved stairway.

Darkness came early with the short December days and lengthened his job of tending the lamp. The fog had closed in early this evening, too, before they'd returned from town. The lamp had already burned steadily for five hours.

Someone hammered on the door. The sound startled him, and he nearly dropped the lid to the oil filter. His heart pounded. It wouldn't be visitors at this hour. Was a ship in trouble? He headed downstairs and cracked the door.

"Rachel!"

He flung the door wide. She was pale and shivering and her blue cloak was damp from the heavy fog. Strands of her auburn hair had come loose from her bun and lay plastered to her skin. She looked wonderful—

better than great. He struggled against the strong urge to crush her to him.

She swept past him and into the parlor to stand near the fire as she fidgeted with the collar of her cloak, undoing the toggle. He glanced out the door once more before closing it, looking for Caleb. "You are alone?"

She nodded. "I have to speak with you. It's urgent. Where's Hannah?"

He helped her with her cloak, surprised to see her dressed in a fancy party dress, but then, everyone had been gone when he dropped by the parsonage earlier to leave the box. "She's in bed with a cold. Nothing serious," he added when she glanced up the stairwell. Her eyes held a certain fearfulness he hadn't seen before. A knot formed in his gut. Something was terribly wrong. "You came all the way out here in the dark? Not an easy thing to do. What has happened?"

"There is a detective in town. He came to our Christmas party this evening looking for a Matthew Taylor. He said that's you."

A chill coursed through him. *Dorian.* "Did he say why he wanted me?"

"For kidnapping, theft and murder."

"Is he on his way here now?"

When he didn't immediately deny the charges, her eyes opened wide.

"No. He'll be here, or the sheriff will, in the morning. Stuart, what have you done?"

He would have done anything to take that stunned look from her face, except lie. He crossed the room and stirred the ashes in the fire, trying to still his chaotic thoughts. Her news, her nearness, played havoc with his concentration. He had to figure out what to do next.

"You're shivering," he said, wishing she'd relax. He opened the trunk at the foot of the stairs and removed a large quilt. As he draped it over her shoulders, he allowed himself the agony of letting his fingers linger for a moment on her smooth skin. She let out a shaky breath and gathered the quilt closer.

"Stuart," she repeated. "What have you done?"

He felt the trap tighten as worry filled her voice. His options? He could run like before. Gather Hannah and be gone within the hour. He met Rachel's eyes and took a deep breath. "So the law has finally caught up with me," he said, his words sounding harsh and callous, even to his ears. "I've done all those things."

She slumped into the nearest chair and covered her face with her hands. "Oh, my God."

He walked to the small window to stare out at the night. He didn't want to see the moment she started hating him—or worse—started fearing him. The smart thing to do would be to escape before the sheriff arrested him. He could pack a few belongings and leave with Hannah before dawn. Maybe take her up the coast to Saunders's place. Dorian had set the hounds on him once before and he'd managed to evade the detectives. He had no doubt that he could do it again. Leaving might be harder on Hannah, though. The lighthouse was her home now. She would have to leave behind things that mattered to her—friends, toys. How many times had he told her not to collect things? They'd only tie her down, make her miserable when it was time to leave.

And now they had tied him, as well. He turned to see Rachel watching him silently, waiting for him to explain. The thought of leaving her hurt beyond all else. Looking back, he could see there were times he could have stopped her visits—should have stopped her visits. He remembered the moment in the kitchen when she had looked upon him, not as Hannah's father or as the light keeper, but as a man. He should have stopped the tutoring then. Instead he had chosen to ignore the warning. He'd been too caught up in how good it felt to be cared for. Didn't she realize she was the one who could stop him?

It seemed as though an eternity passed before he heard her speak. "I don't believe you."

He stared at her.

"I don't believe you. You must have had good reason if you were forced to take such actions. You wouldn't knowingly commit murder. Everything you have done since I met you makes a lie of your admission— rescuing Benjamin, caring for Hannah, refusing to continue the tutoring for fear of my reputation. Everything you do tells me what kind of man you are. There must be a mistake. They want the wrong man."

Her perception of him was so slanted. He wasn't this knight she had somehow painted in her mind. "You've heard the rumors. Your faith in me is misplaced."

Her stubborn reply came quickly from her lips and thundered through the stillness of the room. "No. It's not."

A weary sigh escaped him. This was crazy. He should see her home—at least to the edge of town— then come back and pack.

Her eyes glistened with unshed tears. "What have you done that was so awful? Why can't you tell me? I think I deserve your honesty."

She was right. He was being a beast—and would be more of one once she found he'd run. He'd leave her just like the other men in her life who should have stayed, confirming to her that no one cared enough to think of her, to look out for her. He walked up and placed his hands on her shoulders, softening his voice. "Don't cry, Rachel. I made this mess. I'm only sorry I've dragged you into it."

She wiped furiously at her eyes and stood to face him. "I wanted so badly for you to deny it."

Slowly he raised his hand to the curve of her cheek. "You came here to warn me, and I thank you. But you've taken too many risks for me."

She trembled. "What will become of Hannah if the sheriff takes you away?"

He didn't plan to let that happen. "Don't worry," he murmured and moved closer. "I'll think of something." Gently he tilted her face toward his, searching her eyes.

"Stu…"

He bent down. He needed her, needed this. "No more words Rachel. No words." And he took her mouth, salty in tears, tenderly with his.

Her heart hammered in her chest as he deepened the kiss. He claimed her with his mouth, pulling her gently toward him, setting in motion something she could no longer deny. In her heart she didn't believe his guilt—couldn't believe it. She trembled at his closeness, the possessive strength of his hand on the small of her back as he drew her against him and wrapped his arms around her.

She closed her eyes, melting against him like butter on warm bread, every muscle dissolving until she was sure she'd end up a puddle on the floor if not for his strong embrace. His mouth burned hot against her cold lips. This was what she wanted, and yet…something wasn't right.

He slipped his hand within the folds of her quilt, to the curve of her waist.

She tensed. And everything jolted into place. She wasn't some brainless young schoolgirl to let her body shut out the warning in her mind. She pushed away from him. "The truth," she said, her voice unsteady at first, then stronger. "I want the truth. Tell me about the murder, the kidnapping—all of it."

He stared at her for a full moment. "All right, we'll talk. But you must promise me that when I'm done you'll head back to town."

"I promise."

He turned away, distancing himself. "I didn't kill Linnea if that's what you're thinking."

She stilled at his words.

"I didn't kill her. I told you how that happened."

"The storm at sea. You tried to rescue her…." she prompted.

"I tried—and failed. I couldn't help them both. Together, they were too much for me. The sea was so rough."

It wasn't making sense to her. "But that isn't murder!

You made the only decision you could have. Hannah was the weaker of the two. You had to take the chance that Linnea could help herself. Besides, you said she let go. *She* let go. But you did all you could. And as for the ship—that's not even theft. It was an accident. The cargo—" She stopped, suddenly realizing that she wasn't letting him get a word in. "I'm sorry. Please go on."

"The *Frisco Maiden* had seen better days, but she was mine. Saunders and I had taken her up and down the coast many times. When she went down, a large amount of Lansing's goods sank with her."

"But that loss couldn't be helped."

"You don't understand the influence Lansing has. Dorian has been searching for me for years. I thought perhaps he had given up, at least I hoped he had. I should have known better." A bitter laugh erupted from deep in his throat.

"Is that why you use the name Stuart instead of Matthew?"

He shook his head. "The men on my ship knew me as Stuart but Dorian always insisted on calling me Matthew."

"Always? I don't understand."

"He took me on as a cabin boy when I was ten. My parents were acquaintances of his. Not quite upper crust, but respectable. Linnea was always around when we were in port, and she and I became good friends. When she was eighteen, Dorian sent her up the coast to a finishing school. I guess he was afraid we were getting too serious."

"You weren't good enough for her?" she repeated.

Stuart shook his head. "While she was in that fancy finishing school, she ran off and married a man against her father's wishes. Although her husband had plenty of money, I think he hoped for a part of her wealth, but Dorian wouldn't acknowledge him or Linnea. When Hannah came along, Linnea's husband started to drink more. He was an ugly drunk and took out his ill humor on his family. Linnea was frightened and took Hannah to Dorian hoping to find safety. But he turned her away."

Stuart had been staring at the fire as he talked. Now he looked at her. "Funny. Dorian always drilled into me that a man takes care of his own. Yet when Linnea needed him, he refused her. I could never forgive him for that. Neither could she."

He turned back to the fire. "Then one night Linnea showed up at my ship. She was covered with scrapes and bleeding. Her husband had beaten her and then slapped Hannah across the room. Linnea grabbed a gun and shot him. She thought she had killed him and, scared out of her mind, she came to me for help. But she had only wounded him. He followed her to my ship and pointed the gun at her. And so I killed him. I killed the bastard."

Her mind swirled with all he'd told her. "Were there any witnesses? It's not exactly self-defense, but you were protecting Linnea. Surely that would make sense to any judge."

"Not when it was her husband. He had rights over her that I did not. And he had money. Within hours the rumors were flying around San Francisco, rumors saying her husband had been in a jealous rage because I had seduced Linnea. His family was well connected. They didn't care about the truth—they just wanted revenge for the death of their son. Before the authorities could put me in jail, I weighed anchor and left with Linnea and Hannah. And then the storm happened. Perhaps it was God's retribution, but if so, I should have been the one to drown, not Linnea."

Something still didn't sound right to Rachel. "Why would Dorian charge you with stealing his cargo when the storm caused the accident?"

"He's not interested in the cargo I lost. He accepts losses as a part of his business. That's not the reason he has hunted me down these past three years. He doesn't care about catching me."

"Then why?"

"What he wants is another daughter to replace the one he lost." He met her gaze. "He wants Hannah."

"Hannah!" Her mind reeled with the sudden realization that Hannah was not Stuart's daughter, in fact had never been his daughter. Stuart would never let go of Hannah. But then, Hannah wasn't really his child.

"I promised Linnea I'd watch out for her daughter. I won't go back on my word."

"But Dorian is her grandfather. He has rights too."

Stuart scowled. "He gave them up when he turned Linnea away."

How could one man have so much power that he would use it to destroy another's life? In the end it would hurt Hannah more than anyone. She had lost her mother so violently and now she would face the very real possibility of losing the only man she knew as father too. Agitated, Rachel paced the length of the room and back.

"Stuart. You must leave. Take Hannah and go."

His voice took on a deadly calm. "That was my intention at first. Now, I've changed my mind."

She waited.

"I'm not running."

Her stomach seemed to drop low inside her. "But you said yourself he'll take her! There is time before morning to get away. You can't let him win."

"If I leave here, he's already won."

She stared at him. "What do you mean?"

"I mean that Hannah and I will be looking over our shoulders the rest of our lives. We'll never have peace. I was willing to accept that type of existence before, but no longer. I won't go back to that kind of life."

"None of that will matter if you are in jail and Hannah is with him. I won't—I can't—have the two people I care most about pried apart like some...some clam! You belong together."

The corners of his mouth tilted up in a grim smile. "If I don't face him, I'll never be free."

"You stubborn, stubborn man!" Frustration swept through her even as she understood his reasons for making a stand. She walked to the window and stared out at the mist-ridden blackness.

He was behind her in a second. "Rachel," he murmured, the word muffled into her hair. A shiver coursed through her. "You of all people must understand why I do this. It may be that Hannah will be better off with her grandfather. Dorian has the resources, the doctors and the money to give her the best of help. I know I made that promise to Linnea to keep Hannah and care for her. I've tried to honor it the best I could. But it…it could be I'm hurting her more by holding on."

She turned to face him. "You're wrong. You love her as only a father can. He has no right to Hannah. He turned them away! His own daughter!"

"Shh," he said gently, and gathered her close again, caressing the slope of her shoulder, the curve of her neck. "You've done enough by warning me. I'll consider everything you've said." He smiled grimly. "You do realize that you are an accomplice now?"

"Is that supposed to worry me? It is of no consequence considering what you are going through."

"Perhaps Hannah and I should be gone come morning after all."

She swallowed hard. Morning would come so soon. Too soon. And with it the sheriff or Mr. Pittman. She thought of the note she'd left for the Crouses. She was implicated whether Stuart escaped or whether he stayed put. Either way, she would likely lose her teaching position if she hadn't already. She dragged in a deep breath. This would be her last time alone with Stuart. Nothing mattered but that they were together. She spoke softly into his shirt. "Hold me, Stuart. Please hold me."

His hand stilled on her back.

Slowly she looked up into his eyes. Astonishment showed on his face—and desire.

"Rachel…do you understand what you ask? I can't

just hold you. I...I want you too badly. And I can't promise you any type of a future with me." He looked away, his voice low. "I'd be no better than the other man who left you."

"No. That's not true" she said, thinking how different the two men were. "Joseph had the choice to stay and wouldn't. You don't have that. Tomorrow you'll either be behind bars or gone. I can't change that." She cupped his cheek, pulling his gaze back to hers. "I may lack experience in these matters, Stuart. I...I have never lain with a man. But I am not naive. I know what I'm asking you. I understand the consequences. Even so, I would have this night."

The words were barely off her lips when his mouth slammed into hers. He crushed her to him, deepening the kiss. She opened her mouth to his tongue, and fire exploded through her blood, setting all her nerves on end.

He slipped her dress off her shoulders and trailed kisses down her neck, his breath warm against her cool skin. Shivers raced down her body to her core. She would have melted into the floor had he not held her tight against him. He pulled away and she drew in a shaky breath. "Come with me," he murmured, holding out his hand.

Although her legs felt weak, she followed him.

"Wait here," he instructed at the base of the stairs. In the kitchen he lit a tallow candle, then came back to grasp her hand. His eyes glittered with desire in the light of the flame.

Slowly, holding the candle in front of him, he

climbed the circular stairs. He led her into his bedroom and closed the door, then crossed to his nightstand to set the candle down. "I want you, Rachel. I've wanted you for so long." He turned to face her. "But if you tell me to stop, I will."

She shook her head. She had never been more certain. "I won't change my mind. There will be no regrets come morning. And whatever happens after…"

She let the words trail off as she stepped toward him and slowly unbuttoned his shirt. She could feel his gaze on her face as each button gave way and his shirt finally fell to the floor. Sliding her hands over his warm chest, she felt the strong, steady beat of his heart, heard his sharp intake of breath. She leaned closer and kissed the dark-brown hair sprinkled between his nipples. She raised her face to look at him, and then his mouth was on hers.

His lips slanted across hers, sucking first her lower lip and then her upper one. He teased her with his tongue, flicking across the fullness of her lips and then plunged inside, claiming her. Gone was any thought of the outside world. She wanted only this moment, only this intensity that Stuart could give her. With his hands splayed against the bedroom door, he pressed her back against the wood, his warm body heavy against her.

She arched against him, wanting him closer yet, her breath coming faster and deeper. She pulled his face down so that she could kiss him as thoroughly as he had her, and saw his scar. Tenderly she kissed the puckered skin and then trailed kisses down along the firm line of his jaw, delighting in the roughness of his day-old whiskers and the safety she felt within the circle of his arms.

He picked her up in one fluid motion and strode to the bed. Settling her on his lap, he rained kisses down her throat and across her chest, pushing her damp hair over her shoulder. Her bodice gave way under his fingers and suddenly she was in her chemise, his mouth hot against the cotton material, nuzzling through to her breast. Her nipple responded, puckering in the warm dampness. Her heart hammered as she untied the small bow at the gathered neckline and loosened the material farther.

He slipped his hand beneath the cotton and grasped her breast, molding its softness with his fingers. His breath caught, and he leaned forward to kiss her again. She trembled, moaning into his mouth as waves of desire raced from her breast down through her center. The exquisite torture she felt while he placed light kisses on her neck had her squirming to offer him more flesh. When he finally arrived to suckle at her breast she spread her fingers through his thick dark hair, and let her head fall back in complete surrender.

He moaned and shifted, moving to catch her other nipple between his lips and give it equal attention. Against her buttocks she felt the firm rise of his body and pressed against him, reveling in the sensations that pulsed through her core.

She drew the chemise over her head, before him naked and trembling—although not from the cold.

"You're so beautiful," he said, his voice hoarse. "In the candlelight—you glow."

Pleasure suffused her. She couldn't take her eyes from him either—his dark hair tousled from her fingers, the seductive shadows and valleys of the muscles across his chest and shoulders, the strong line of his jaw. In the flickering candlelight his skin shone a pale gold.

He moved her from his lap and then removed his pants. She caught just a glimpse of him before he pulled her into his bed. A thrill rushed through her. She snuggled against him and caressed the width of his back and down his arms, enjoying the feel of his firm muscles, the exquisite pleasure of her skin molding to his, thigh to thigh, breast to chest.

He groaned, and with the sound a feeling of power came over her. "Oh, Stuart," she sighed into his ear and kissed the soft lobe. "I want your touch as much as you want me—probably more."

"That's impossible," he murmured, rising on one elbow and pushing a strand of her hair away from her cheek. Looking directly into her eyes, he moved her beneath him, grinding his firmness against her pelvis. She gasped as pleasure exploded through her body, her eyelids drifting closed to block out everything but the sensation. Her skin tingled as he smoothed his hand along her torso, down her hips, between her thighs.

She moaned and arched up against his fingers, opening her legs farther, longing for his entry. Wanting him. "I...I need you," she whispered against his neck.

"Shh. I know." He met her gaze. "You're so beautiful, Rachel. So damn beautiful." He took her mouth once again with his, moved on top of her and then thrust himself into her body, stifling her sudden outcry with his kiss. She clung to him, barely breathing as he paused, letting the sensual feelings race over them both. Then the sweet rhythm of his body pushing into hers, deeper and deeper, carried her away until she lost all thought and could only feel and respond in kind.

Time slipped away and her world became his world. A small, candlelit room that shut out the cold and wind and dark. He was her refuge, her warmth, her desire. She strained against him, asking for more with her body, wanting him closer, deeper inside. The sensation built until her body bucked and she gripped him tight as wave after wave of feeling overwhelmed her.

"You're mine now," he gasped and shuddered into her with such force, it took her over the edge of all feeling. Then he collapsed on her, breathing hard, his energy spent as he wrapped his arms around her.

She felt his heart beating against hers, the rhythm slowing, and drew comfort from him. She wanted this to last forever, this feeling of safety and caring and contentment. Knowing it wouldn't brought the sting of tears to her eyes.

He rose up on his elbows over her, then leaned down and kissed the wetness, his lips tender. "I'll remember this moment forever," he murmured against her ear.

And then he held her, as she'd asked.

Stuart lay awake as the gray light of dawn seeped through the window, wondering how things would play out today of all days. Rachel snuggled deeper into his arms, her backside flush against him. He chuckled into her hair and kissed the nape of her neck. She had given him such a gift last night.

The thundering report of a harpoon gun echoed loudly through the small room, the sound shaking the small window.

Rachel tensed and her eyes flew open.

"The Johnson Company—after a whale. Probably their last one." He smoothed back the tendrils of hair on her forehead as he felt her relax back into his pillow. He sighed. "And my notice to get moving." Turning away from her, he climbed reluctantly from the bed.

"Not yet, Stuart. Come back."

He smiled, but continued to pull on his pants and chambray shirt. "You make it hard to leave the bed, but I need to put out the light."

She groaned into the pillow and then stretched languorously. The wool cover slipped, revealing a soft breast.

His breath caught at the sight. She was beautiful, lying there, her dark-auburn hair spread over the pillow. He swallowed hard, wanting nothing more than to lose himself in her again. Instead he stepped away from the bed.

"Hannah will be up soon. I doubt your being here would upset her, but the sheriff might react differently."

She squeezed her eyes shut. "The sheriff! Oh, Stuart. You should have left…you should have gone," she moaned. "Perhaps there is still time?"

He shook his head. "It's time to face the consequences. That became clear last night."

She sighed, meeting his gaze. "Everything will change now."

He understood. Everything had changed. He left the room to begin his duties with the light.

Downstairs she was making coffee when he came into the room and walked up to wrap his arms around her waist. The party dress from last night was wrinkled, her hair was loose, and she had a well-satisfied look about her. She couldn't look more stunning. He breathed deeply against her hair. "Did you find the box?"

"It's beautiful. Thank you." She poured some coffee into a mug and turned around, handing it to him. "Tell Hannah thank you."

"You can tell her yourself. She is stirring." He took a sip. "Much better than mine."

She poured herself a cup. "I do have one question about all you said last night."

He smiled. "Only one?"

She returned his smile and elbowed him. "How did you get the job here? Surely the lighthouse board hired you without knowing your past."

"Someone owed Saunders a favor."

"You and this Saunders must be very close."

Stuart put down his mug. "We go way back. I'm fortunate to call him a friend."

"I suppose you can call me a friend too," Rachel said, a teasing light coming into her eyes.

"We passed that point long ago. And last night... well, last night proved it." He pulled her to his chest and kissed her thoroughly. She returned his kiss with matching ardor, until he knew the moment her legs gave way and she began to sink. He pulled her up, reluctantly moving to kiss her cheeks, her face and her neck. He breathed her scent, then whispered in her ear,

"Rachel, we have to stop or Hannah will find both of us on the floor."

She stumbled back from him and dragged in a deep breath. "You're right, of course."

He nearly grabbed her to him again, she looked so beautiful and disheveled, her eyes misty. He searched his mind for something to keep his mind off her lips and his hands off her body. "I saw the article in the paper. Caleb brought it out. How bad has it been for you in town?"

She didn't speak for a moment. "I'm handling it. Mrs. Crouse says it will blow over."

"You're a strong woman."

"I don't feel very strong. At least not right now." Her voice trembled. "The school board has suspended me from teaching."

"Oh, Rachel. I'm sorry." He sure had messed up her life along with his. What would happen over the next week or month? Would she come to hate him? He'd deserve it if she did.

She drew in a shaky breath. "Well, at least now they have a valid reason to keep me from influencing their children."

He frowned. "What happened last night was wonderful—not wrong. It could never be wrong." He took her by the shoulders and looked deep into her eyes. "You are worth staying for. Believe that."

Her gaze skittered away. "I don't have much experience with people staying, Stuart. You know that."

He wanted to punch the men who'd done that to her—made her feel as though she were unworthy. They were the ones who'd been wrong…and selfish. He touched her chin, turning her to face him. "I wish I could promise you I'd be here tomorrow. But I can't."

"I know." The words were barely a whisper.

"No regrets, remember?"

"No regrets."

A loud pounding vibrated the lighthouse door.

Chapter Nineteen

Stuart waited a moment, giving Rachel time to collect herself. Then he opened the door to Sheriff Thorne and Terrance. As one, the two men looked from Stuart's face, past him, to see Rachel.

"I see there is no need to explain why I'm here," Sheriff Thorne said.

Terrance's eyes narrowed suspiciously on her face. In the harsh morning light, Stuart saw distinctly when Morley noticed her heightened color, the puffiness in her lips. With an enraged snarl, Terrance sprung forward and rammed his fist into Stuart's face.

Pain exploded in his nose and cheek. Stuart staggered back, blood spurting from his nose and coating his lips.

Rachel raced across the room toward him, but stopped abruptly when he straightened and put out a warning hand to her to stay out of the way.

"Maybe I deserved that," he said in a low controlled voice. "But I won't take it. Not from you, Morley."

"You deserve much worse!" Terrance hauled back his fist, preparing to strike again.

"No!" Rachel screamed. *"Stop!"*

Terrance struck down.

Stuart blocked with his arm, at the same time plowing his fist into Terrance's gut. With a loud whoosh, air exploded from Terrance's lungs and he landed in a heap on the floor.

"That'll be enough from both of you," Sheriff Thorne said, pushing them apart, his hand on his gun.

Stuart staggered back a step and then regained his balance. He straightened slowly, keeping one eye on Terrance and the other on the sheriff and his gun. The metallic taste of blood tinged his mouth.

Terrance caught his breath, propped himself up on his elbow and glared from Stuart to Rachel, but it seemed the fight was out of him. His eyes narrowed on Rachel and a look of disgust crossed his face.

Stuart would have done anything to knock that look off his face. With a growl he started toward him, grabbed his collar and hauled him to his feet.

"Hold on!" the sheriff barked, and swung Stuart around, jabbing the gun into his ribs. Blood splattered from Stuart's nose over Terrance.

"Don't move, Taylor. Git me a rag, Miss Houston."

The alarm in Rachel's eyes stopped him from jerking out of the sheriff's grip and tearing Terrance apart. He quieted as she grabbed a cloth from the cabinet. The sheriff whipped it out of her hand and threw it at Stuart.

"Take care of your nose. You're gushing every-where." He turned back to Rachel. "Mrs. Crouse put a package for you in my saddlebag. You are to open it now."

She nodded as if in a daze and stepped outside.

The sheriff turned to Stuart. "You know why I'm here. No dancin' around the cow as they say. Collect your things, Taylor. The logbook too. And get the girl ready."

"Where's this detective?"

"He's waiting at the jail. Didn't want to dirty his hands if you put up a fight."

"That's noble of him," Stuart said, sarcasm ripe in his voice.

"Humph," the sheriff huffed.

"I don't plan to give you any trouble, Sheriff. Only if Morley gives me more grief." He turned and headed up the stairs. Hannah had heard the commotion, and he found her sitting in bed, the quilt covers up to her nose, her gray eyes big.

"It's okay, Hannah. Get dressed. We're going into town." He gathered her few clothes and bundled them together. While she dressed herself, he went into his bedroom and got his few things together.

When he returned downstairs with Hannah, Rachel had changed from her party dress into the yellow everyday dress he'd seen before. Her hair was still down, tousled over her shoulders. She looked pale, shaken.

"Mrs. Crouse's package," she said, indicating her dress. "I tied up the puppy and gave him food and water. Caleb can come out later to keep an eye on things."

Silently he nodded his thanks.

Thorne watched him closely. "Saw your name in the newspaper. Quite a hero, you and Caleb."

"Neither one of us wanted that story in the paper, Sheriff. I think you can figure out why."

Thorne nodded. "It hasn't gone easy for Miss Houston. When the townsfolk found out she came out here so much, they suspended her from her teaching position."

"She told me."

"It was just until the school board's next meeting," Terrance said. "But now…"

Stuart met his gaze. "I hired Miss Houston to tutor my daughter. Nothing more."

"That doesn't change the fact that she raced out here last night to warn you and then stayed," Terrance said stonily. "Although, maybe we should thank her. She probably kept you from running when you had the chance."

Stuart glanced at Rachel. She was so still that he knew she believed what Terrance had said.

"Yes," Sheriff Thorne said. "I've been thinking about that myself. Why didn't you run, Taylor?"

Stuart shrugged. He wasn't about to go into something that personal with these two. "I have my reasons, Sheriff. But I guess I should get a lawyer, or at least wait until Dorian arrives and I have a better idea where things stand."

"That may be best. A few things just don't add up here and I'd like to get to the bones of it. Officially I am arresting you for kidnapping and possible murder." Thorne stood and then glanced at Hannah. "You got any kin around that could watch the girl?"

"No."

"Mrs. Baier might take her in at the boarding house."

He scratched his temple. "What about Miss Houston? Seein' as how she's been tutoring the girl…"

"Rachel could lose her job permanently. No, she's done enough for us as it is."

Terrance shook his head with disgust. "Interesting how you seem to care so much now that it won't help. Her reputation is ruined."

It was all he could do to keep from beating Morley to a pulp. "Her reputation is only ruined if you or Sheriff Thorne mention her being here last night. I'm sure the Crouses won't. The school board doesn't have to know."

Terrance snorted. "In a town this size? The whole thing will be impossible to keep quiet."

He hated to ask, but he'd do it for Rachel if it would help. "If you really care about her, why don't you bring her into town in another hour, rather than have her ride in with the Sheriff and me?"

Stony silence met his request.

Rachel stepped forward. "At this point, town gossip is the least of my worries, Stuart. But perhaps it would be easier for Hannah to ride with me. And I do want her to stay with me at the parsonage."

He stared at her a long time before answering. It was what he wanted. Hannah would be frightened in a strange place all alone. And he couldn't bear the thought of either one of them watching him ride into town and being jailed. "All right."

"What about the light?" Thorne asked.

"You'll have to contact the lighthouse board when we get to town. Caleb knows how to manage the light if you'll trust him."

"He's kind of young," said Thorne, rubbing his chin. "But all right. Let's go. You coming, Morley?"

Again Terrance met Stuart's gaze. "I'll start back with Miss Houston and the girl in half an hour."

Hannah ran to Stuart then and threw her arms around him. He crouched down on one knee in order to hug her back. She clung hard, locking her fingers together behind his neck. Stuart squeezed his eyes shut to keep the sudden moisture in check. It wouldn't do to show any signs of weakness—not in front of Rachel. And this was probably the last time he'd see Hannah. The thought staggered him. How could he live with himself?

"Time to go," Thorne said again and tried to pull Hannah away, but she held on tighter. "Taylor…" Warning crept into his voice.

"All right, Sheriff. Hannah, stay with Rachel for now." He talked softly, reassuring her, all the while prying her fingers away one at a time. Tears rolled down her soft cheeks, making his chest ache. This is how he'd remember her.

He pressed her hand into Rachel's and squeezed. Then, standing, he looked at Rachel hard, memorizing the way she looked—her hair down about her shoulders, wavy and curled slightly at the ends, her lips puffy from their last kiss, her green eyes luminous. He said firmly, "Don't come to the jail."

Then he turned and stepped outside with Sheriff Thorne. They walked to the shed and he saddled Blanco under Thorne's vigilant gun. When he was settled on the horse, Thorne reached into his pocket and pulled out handcuffs.

Stuart swallowed hard. This was it.

He steadied his gaze on the sheriff. "I won't run, you know. I would have been gone by now if that's how I wanted to handle this."

"I figured that. But I don't plan on making any mistakes. And who's to know if you should change your mind about coming peacefully once we get closer to town? Here. Put your hands out."

Stuart hesitated. There would be no chance of turning back after this. He took a deep breath and held out his arms.

Chapter Twenty

Ping!

Rachel glanced out the kitchen window to see Caleb practicing in the backyard with his pellet gun. The frequent clatter of a tin can falling from the fence proved how good a shot he had become since Sam gave him the gun as a gift. The last of Settie's puppies darted under his feet and dashed about the yard in a circle, yipping and barking at the noisy cans.

She turned back to the table and finished quartering the potatoes for supper, her thoughts scattered, sometimes worried, sometimes angry but always on Stuart. The stubborn, mule-headed man! He was so close—just around the square—and she wanted to go to him. She had struggled for the past three days over doing just that.

The church door slammed, and Reverend Crouse crossed the lawn. He stopped and watched Caleb knock down two more cans. "It will be dark before long. You should leave for the lighthouse. Make yourself ready."

"Yes sir." Caleb followed Reverend Crouse into the kitchen.

"I have a satchel for you," Rachel said, motioning to the cloth bag on the table. "Enough for two days, at least. You should be able to find more in the pantry there."

"Thanks, sis."

"Are you managing out there?"

"Sure. It's quiet, but that's okay. Sam's coming out to visit tomorrow. We might do a little fishing—from the rock."

Reverend Crouse handed Caleb a box of matches. "It is a man's job you are doing. Hopefully, the board will find a replacement soon."

"I know how to work the light," Caleb said, throwing a frustrated glance at them both. "I've seen Mr. Taylor do it before."

Reverend Crouse smiled. "I don't doubt that you do. I am worried that you will be called upon to do more rescuing if a ship comes to trouble."

Rachel hugged her brother. "Be careful, Caleb."

He grinned and settled his hat on his head. Nodding to them both, he ducked out the kitchen door and headed for the carriage house where Stuart's horse was now kept.

Rachel turned back to the table and began slicing the carrots for the stew. Her brother was looking forward to proving himself. He viewed this as a challenge. She wouldn't have thought him capable of handling the responsibility six months ago, but a lot had happened since the picnic and Benjamin's fall. Caleb had grown up quite a bit and she— Well, she had fallen in love.

"Oh!" Stinging pain radiated through her hand. Blood dripped from the cut on her finger. She dropped the knife, sending it clattering across the floor and grabbed her apron to apply pressure to the cut.

"What happened?" Emma asked, coming through the kitchen door and looking from her husband to Rachel. "Dear, are you all right?"

"Yes," Rachel murmured, hunching her shoulders. Emma stepped closer and reached for her injured hand.

Rachel jerked away, but couldn't keep her eyes from filling with tears.

Emma took one look at Rachel's face and shooed her husband from the room. "Supper will be a while yet. I'll help." She pulled out a chair for Rachel, pushed her into it and then began cutting the celery for the pot. "Now, you sit there and tell me all that's bothering you, Rachel."

"I said I'm fine."

"Well, I'll believe that when there is a smile on your face, but not now."

Emma had always been kind, but in light of all the snubbing Rachel had endured, it meant so much now. She rewrapped her finger with her apron and squeezed until it went numb, wishing she could do the same to her heart. "Everything is such a mess," she said, and felt hot tears spill over.

Emma pulled out her handkerchief and dabbed at Rachel's face. "I've been around a bit longer than you. Perhaps I can help you muddle through some of your mess."

* * *

Early that evening Terrance surprised her with a visit.

"We need to talk," he said, standing in the parlor, holding Rachel's cloak open for her. "Let's take a walk."

Since returning from the lighthouse she had stayed inside, going out only for necessities. "I don't know, Terrance. The way things have been it's not a good idea."

Terrance's smile turned impatient. "I've had time to calm down, to think through a few things and I believe I deserve a chance to have my say."

Still she hesitated.

"I want to discuss the things those on the school board are saying."

Reluctantly Rachel tugged her cloak about her neck and hooked the toggles. Terrance's mood worried her and she wasn't sure she wanted to hear what he had to say. After all, he had been the one to relay information to that detective. He'd had a hand in Stuart's arrest.

Purposely she started off in the direction away from the jail. They walked around the Custom House, down Talbot Street toward the livery. Lanterns glowed in several of the houses and she saw one figure watching through an open window. A dog barked from a darkened porch as they passed, and one impudent skunk slowly walked across the road in front of them. At the schoolhouse, Terrance stopped her. He'd been quiet, unusual for him.

"Still wishing you could teach?"

She nodded.

"I know you don't want to hear this, but you need to be realistic now."

"What do you mean?"

He met her eyes. "Do you think people here would want you teaching their children now that they know what has happened?"

"And what exactly has happened?"

"You know what I mean. Most of the town has heard one version or another of your exploits."

"My exploits!" A sarcastic laugh escaped before she could clamp her mouth shut tight. "What are they saying?"

"It isn't funny," Terrance said. "I don't like what they're saying about you, whether you care or not."

"I do care. It's just that there is nothing I can do about it. Nothing I say will change their minds. It is the mob mentality."

He grasped her hand, tucked it in the crook of his arm and patted it. "In a week Taylor and Hannah will both be gone. And you are the one who will still be here fending off the rumors."

"A sadder but wiser girl, is that it?"

They walked on in uneasy silence, his words troubling her. They retraced their steps past the church and the parsonage, until they finally came to the jail. Terrance's grip on her hand tightened as they strolled by the darkened windows. Each step echoed loudly on the wooden boardwalk. Her spine stiffened. She refused to look, refused to wonder whether Stuart saw her.

At the edge of town near the new wharf, Terrance stopped and looked across the harbor. A few isolated lights twinkled in the distance, ten miles away in New San Diego. Water slapped against the rocks at her feet.

Terrance faced her and sighed. "I've been angry. Very angry. I needed a few days to sort through things."

"And have you?"

"Enough to know that I want to make things work between us."

Rachel pulled back. This was the last thing she expected to hear from him. "Terrance. There is no 'us.'"

"I'm not a fool. I know you don't feel the same way about me. I just thought I could help you through some of this. Maybe still take you into San Diego for your teaching exam."

She studied his long face, his mud-colored eyes that watched her so closely. "You'd do that for me? After all that has happened?"

"You should have something to think about. Something to take your mind off Taylor. It's time to get on with your life."

His thoughtfulness confused her after the way he'd acted at the lighthouse. "I never thanked you for accompanying me home the other morning."

"That's easily remedied."

She looked up and suddenly he was kissing her, his lips hard against hers, his oiled mustache brushing her cheeks. When he pressed his entire length against her she broke away, shaking. "Stop, Terrance."

His voice came low and angry. "You were happy enough to take Taylor's kisses. Mine aren't good enough for you?"

The hair on the back of her neck prickled, and the first inklings of fear crept into her. She stepped back. "I want to go home now." When he didn't move, she forced a calm she didn't feel and said firmly, "I mean it, Terrance. Take me home."

"Not until I get a proper kiss from you." He grabbed her shoulders and pulled her toward him.

She struggled, trying to loosen his grip, but he was too strong for her. He crushed his mouth against hers and forced her lips apart, invading her with his tongue.

Suddenly he released her. "Daughter of a gold panner," he said with derision. "You could have been so much more."

She stumbled back and wiped her bruised mouth. "Never touch me again, Mr. Morley. Never." Then she turned and strode toward the parsonage.

He'd seen enough—the kiss, the embrace. Stuart turned away from the jail's window, the sight of Rachel and Terrance too much to bear. He gripped the black iron bars tighter, in his mind reliving the satisfied smirk Terrance had tossed in his direction when he walked by with Rachel on his arm. Stuart wanted to strangle him. It twisted his gut to see another man with her.

Especially Terrance.

With a growl he turned from the window and paced the length of his cell, and for the hundredth time he questioned if he had done the right thing in staying.

He'd heard and seen plenty his first few days in jail.

Amanda Furst visited the mercantile daily, mostly to flirt with Terrance, her high-pitched giggle drifting across the street and grating on Stuart's nerves. Samuel had come to visit once along with his parents. They had offered him a reward for saving Sam's life—money he could use to purchase the services of a lawyer.

He welcomed the day that Dorian would arrive and put an end to this purgatory. Anything was better than what he suffered now.

If only…

He clamped down on the thought. No point in dwelling on what couldn't be. He plopped down on the cot and glanced at the window. Rachel had already paid dearly. And it was his fault…his fault! He smashed his fist into the thin pillow.

Chapter Twenty-One

Four days later, the sky spit rain from leaden clouds as a team of dapple-gray horses pulled a private coach to a stop in front of the small jail. Stuart rose from his cot and peered through the iron bars of the window that faced the street. A tall, thin man stepped down to the dusty street and paused to glance about the town. In his hand he grasped the ivory-handled cane he carried with him at all times—more for a display of power than for any need of assistance to walk.

The old ambivalence resurfaced while Stuart watched. He could well imagine the man's musings, probably comparing the haphazard array of wooden slapped-up buildings against the solid structures of San Francisco. Most likely anger built as he assessed the kind of place his granddaughter had lived in for the past year, and found everything wanting.

The years had changed him. The gray fox eyes seemed just as bright, just as startling as they once had, but the silver hair combed straight back from his forehead had thinned, with white scalp showing through at the temple. He still held himself straight and rigid, like he had when he walked the deck of his own ship and was used to having everyone obey his slightest command. He adjusted his coat more comfortably over his narrow shoulders, settled his stovepipe hat on his head and strode into the jail.

Stuart moved to watch the sheriff and Dorian through the small barred opening. Thorne studied the stranger from underneath the low brim of his Stetson. He leaned back in his chair and chewed on a stalk of winter grass. Stuart had witnessed a couple of his run-ins over the past week and wondered now who would have the upper hand. The outcome would make an interesting wager if he were a betting man, but either way he was bound to end up the loser in this game.

Dorian tapped his cane against the floorboards, two sharp staccato beats that sent dust flying and commanded the sheriff's attention. He removed his tall hat with a flourish and tucked it against his waistcoat. "Good day. I understand you are holding a prisoner for me?"

"Well now, that depends on who you are," Sheriff Thorne said.

"Dorian Lansing, merchant and sole proprietor of Lansing Enterprises of San Francisco. I was informed by telegraph that you had arrested Matthew Taylor. I came at my earliest opportunity. He is here, is he not?"

"He's here all right. I'll need some identification before you can see him. Also, you'll have to remove any weapons or firearms. You can understand that, I'm sure."

"Of course. And might I know your name for my records?"

Stuart leaned against the bars, watching. Dorian was always primed for a power struggle. The sheriff drew in a long, slow breath and leaned forward on his seat, hands on his knees, belly protruding over his wide leather belt.

"It's Thorne—Randolph Thorne. T-h-o-r-n-e. Got that?"

Dorian's steel-gray eyes didn't blink but drew into slits as he looked over the sheriff. "Thank you, Sheriff Thorne. Here are my papers."

He withdrew a small packet of papers from his waist-coat pocket and dropped them on the desk. Thorne looked them over for a full minute before standing and offering them back to Dorian.

"Seem to be in order. Ah…about the firearms."

Dorian unbuttoned his coat and withdrew a derringer from an inside pocket. He placed it carefully on the desk.

"Follow me."

The sheriff took the key ring from its hook and proceeded to the door separating the two rooms. Stuart met his gaze through the small window, tight-lipped and grim, a man doing his duty but not wholly agreeing with the lay of things.

Stuart backed up to his cot and took a deep breath.

The door banged open.

"Visitor for you, Taylor," the sheriff called out.

Dorian walked slowly to the door of the cell, a hard expression on his cosmopolitan face, his cane tapping out a determined third beat to his polished boots. He stopped directly in front of Stuart and studied him through the bars—first his face, then his coarse cotton shirt and Levi's, down to his worn boots and then back to his face.

Stuart couldn't read a thing in the man's gaze. He knew better than to try. So he just stood there, letting the man who had once been like a father to him look his fill, remembering that this man had turned his back on his only daughter in her time of need.

"So," Dorian said at last in a gravelly voice. "I have finally tracked you down."

Stuart remained silent…waiting.

"How long has it been?"

"Three years."

"I doubt I would have found you now had it not been for the newspaper article. Of course, the mercantile owner helped quite a bit, too. I'll have to stop by to thank him personally."

That newspaper article again! It had hurt Rachel and now it had come back to haunt him. Who'd have thought rescuing three men in a boat would be the bait to ruin his life?

"I was happy enough to know where you had stolen my granddaughter off to."

Stuart's hold on his temper slipped. "You turned your back on her and her mother."

"You and I both know that is not the case. I was trying to make my daughter see the error of her ways. The choices she made were her downfall."

"Twist it any way you like. You're still wrong."

"Well, now we come to it," Dorian said.

Fear rose like bile in Stuart's throat. If Dorian challenged Stuart's right to Hannah, he would win.

Dorian sighed and spoke to him as though to a child. "Hannah is not your flesh and blood. She's my daughter's child but not yours. You have no right to her."

"My right comes by way of Linnea." He'd failed Linnea before, he wouldn't let this go without a fight. "She wanted me to raise Hannah. Not you. It was the last thing she asked of me."

"Well, things have changed considerably since that time. Hannah will be the sole surviving heir of Lansing Enterprises. She needs to be brought up properly, according to her station."

"So that's why you manufactured the kidnapping charge."

"Along with the loss of the cargo. It proved a convenient way to cast a net to pull you in. The murder charge— well that will be settled in court. You did a deep disservice to me when you ran off that night. And, I might add, Rose has never been the same since. Under the circumstances, there is little to commend you as a merchant—or a father."

Stuart glared at the man before him. "I learned from the best."

Dorian looked shaken for a moment, for once unsure of how to proceed. He sank down on the bench along the wall and sighed.

"You are not going to win this time, Matthew," he said in a low voice, his hands clenched together on the knob of his cane. "You took my only daughter from me. You will not have my granddaughter, too."

"Linnea asked me to raise Hannah."

"You turned her head!" Dorian cried out in his gravelly voice. "You used her vulnerability. All you ever wanted was her money, her position. Now look what's become of her. She has the ocean as her grave!"

Stuart rushed to the bars and gripped them tightly. "Never again put me in the same class as the brute she married," he ground out through clenched teeth. "Understand this once and for all. I never cared about her money—your money. That should be evident enough. I have nothing now. Just a lowly job as light keeper. But what I have is mine. And Hannah is *mine!*"

Dorian's eyes narrowed as he said icily. "I may be getting older, but I am no fool."

"What would you know about the feelings we had for each other? Did you ever try to understand your daughter?"

"Don't talk to me about Linnea. If you both had been honest with me none of this would be happening now."

"Is that what this is all about? Honesty? You're angry Linnea ran to me when you refused to help her? I should think you'd thank me! Or are you just irritated she didn't come crawling to you a second time? You always liked being the one with total control."

Dorian had twisted their relationship into something ugly, and Stuart wouldn't have it. He'd had feelings for Linnea from the start—but when she had gone off and married another man he'd come to accept it. He released his grip and turned away from the man who had at one time meant everything to him. "Believe what you will. You've chosen the way you want to see things so that you can justify taking Hannah from me."

"A daughter for a daughter, Matthew."

Stuart stared at Dorian but remained silent.

The small room filled with the oppressive silence of two strong wills, fighting for the thing they considered most dear, one in control, one in despair. After a while, Dorian rose to his feet.

"Where is she?" he said in a low voice.

Stuart wouldn't answer.

"So be it," Dorian said. "You'll be tried in San Francisco in two weeks."

"How convenient. A place where you can line the pockets of the lawyers and judge. The charges?"

"Kidnapping, theft and the murder of John Newcomb." He strode out of the room, slamming the door on his way.

As Dorian tapped by the window and climbed into the coach, Stuart pushed his face against the cold iron bars. "You may take Hannah, thinking in some crooked way that it's justified for the life of your daughter, but you'll be wrong. I pity you, Dorian. Do you hear me? You're a sad, old man."

Chapter Twenty-Two

Rachel removed the towel covering a large earthenware bowl and leaned over to see how much the dough had risen. The afternoon sun slanted through the kitchen window, refusing to give off much warmth this time of year, but it had done its job with the dough. Hannah sat on a high stool watching the proceedings with interest, every so often turning to Emma, who sat beside her, trying to learn the finger alphabet.

A sharp double knock came at the front door.

Emma rose. "I'll answer it."

Voices came from the other room as Rachel continued working the dough. Emma returned with a sad look on her face. "He's here."

Rachel's heart dropped to her stomach. Dorian. She glanced at Hannah and tried to smile before following Emma into the parlor.

A tall, wiry stranger, stylishly dressed beyond anything she'd seen in La Playa, sat in the wingback chair. He cradled his hat in his lap and turned the rim—

whether out of boredom or a case of nerves, Rachel wasn't sure. When she approached, he stood.

"I'm Hannah Taylor's grandfather, Dorian Lansing, and I've come to take her home with me."

Even though she'd expected it, Rachel still wasn't ready for the blow.

"She is living with you, is she not?" Dorian's gaze darted to Mrs. Crouse for confirmation.

"She's here," Rachel answered. "May I see some form of identification?"

"Certainly." Dorian withdrew a packet of papers from his pocket. "This is the second time I've had to verify my identity. That sheriff of yours doesn't leave anything to chance."

"Yes," Rachel said dryly. "We're lucky to have him. I take it you've been to see Mr. Taylor, then."

"Yes. He is aware that I am here for Hannah. These papers assign me authority to take Hannah back to San Francisco."

Rachel looked over the papers and handed them back with a sigh. She had known this time would come, thought she was prepared, but now her heart lodged in her throat and she wanted nothing more than for this cultured stranger to turn around and walk back out the front door.

"We have become rather attached to Hannah in the past week," Emma said, her experience as a pastor's wife coming to the fore as she graciously motioned for Dorian to enter. "She is a good child. Won't you come in?"

"I'll fetch Hannah." Rachel turned and walked slowly

into the kitchen. A smudge of flour slashed across one of Hannah's cheeks, and dashes of the white powder dusted the table and circled the girl's feet. Rachel untied the oversize apron and hugged her. "There is someone here to see you," she said, carefully keeping her voice light. She smoothed Hannah's hair and brushed the flour from her cheek. "Someone from long ago who knew you when you were a baby. Your grandfather, Dorian Lansing."

Hannah's eyes widened with delight. Her first reaction would depend largely on how Rachel handled this herself, so Rachel held her hand reassuringly and led her into the parlor.

Dorian sat down suddenly when they entered the parlor, his stern expression dissolving into one of shock. He stared from under thin black brows at his granddaughter's face. His fingers trembled on the ivory handle of his cane. "She looks like her mother," he said huskily, his face softening. "Come here, child."

Hannah released Rachel's hand and approached him slowly. Rachel could tell she did not remember the man, but she could also see that Hannah was not fearful of him. When she stood, respectfully quiet before Dorian, he suddenly smiled.

"Do you know who I am?"

Hannah glanced at Rachel as if asking permission to answer. Rachel smiled reassuringly. Hannah turned back to the old man and nodded her head.

"I am your mother's father, dear. Your grandfather."

A puzzled frown met his words at the mention of Hannah's mother.

"Have you nothing to say of that, child?"

He waited, expecting an answer. Finally Hannah brought her hands in front of her and signed, "Hello, Grandfather."

Dorian looked to Rachel. "What is this? A game?"

Again Hannah signed, "Hello."

Dorian caught her hands in his large grasp to still them. "Dear. I don't know this game you play. You will have to teach me on our way to San Francisco."

At that, Hannah's eyes grew wary.

"Yes. We are going on a trip. It is time you saw your grandmother Rose. She misses you terribly, just as I have. She will be surprised to see how you resemble your mother. She has been sad a long time, but I'm sure seeing you will cheer her up."

Hannah pulled away from Dorian's grasp and began signing in earnest, her small, slender fingers flying in front of his face.

Dorian's brows drew together in a frown. "Would someone please tell me what is going on here?" he said, impatience creeping into his voice. "I don't have time for these silly games."

The tone stopped Hannah's fingers, and she backed away, an uncertain look on her face.

"You just might want to learn these silly games," Rachel said steadily. She sat in the chair at right angles to Dorian, took a deep breath and smiled at Hannah. Above all, she didn't want the child frightened. "Slow down, Hannah. Start again."

Her fingers slowed, and Rachel caught the idea of what Hannah said.

"She wants to know where San Francisco is,"

Rachel interpreted for Dorian. "And how far it is from here."

Dorian sat back. "She cannot speak?"

"No, not since the accident at sea."

Dorian peered at Hannah for a moment. "Has she been to a doctor? Is there something wrong with her throat?"

"The doctor said her muteness was due to shock, not an injury to the vocal cords. She may regain the use of speech in time or the cords may atrophy and she will never speak."

"Only one doctor? Didn't Matthew get another opinion?"

"He respected this doctor and did not feel the need to go to another to hear the same thing."

"Or have the funds to see to her welfare," Dorian said angrily. He clasped Hannah's hands to his chest, making the girl flinch. "We'll just see about that! I'll have the best doctors this side of the Rockies see her. And if they cannot help her, then I'll take her to Boston myself."

"You would take her that far away?" Rachel asked, a catch in her throat.

"If I have to."

This was all moving too fast. Stuart would never get to see Hannah if Dorian had his way. Surely there could be some compromise.

Hannah began her finger ballet again, this time earnestly watching Rachel's face. When Rachel realized the message, she hesitated at first, and then translated for Dorian. "She wants to know if her father will be coming to San Francisco also."

A frown passed over Dorian's face. "He'll be there, but he can't come with us."

Hannah's fingers flew to their own rhythm again.

"Oh. I don't think so Hannah." Rachel shook her head.

"What?" Dorian sat forward. "What did she just ask?"

Rachel's cheeks warmed. "She asked if I would be going with her."

Dorian's gaze narrowed on her. "Why would she ask that?"

Her breath hitched at the question. She didn't want to reveal anything to this man that he might use against Stuart. "I've been tutoring Hannah for some time now and we've become good friends. My brother and I rode out to the lighthouse to work with her."

Dorian's sharp eyes narrowed as he listened to Rachel. Could he read behind her words? It certainly felt like it. Heat rose in her cheeks. He pulled once at his gray handlebar mustache, reminding her fleetingly of Terrance.

"I appreciate the care you have given Hannah." He rose from the chair and walked to the door. "I'll stay the night at the Horton Grand Hotel in San Diego. I have some shipping business to conclude there. At noon tomorrow, I'll return to fetch Hannah. Please see that her things are packed and ready to go. I'll, ah, have a small donation for the church for the care that you've given her." He nodded to Emma and started for the door.

"Wait! Sir!" Rachel cried out suddenly as a thought came to her.

Dorian stopped in the process of settling his hat on his head. "Yes?"

"You will let Hannah say goodbye to her fa— I mean, Stuart."

Dorian's lips pressed together in displeasure as he looked from Rachel to Hannah. That Hannah understood what was happening was all too evident by the terrified expression on her face.

"He's watched over her for three years," Rachel said, knowing that had Dorian known where Stuart was, those three years would not have happened.

A muscle worked in Dorian's jaw. "I'll let her say goodbye." The door closed with a soft thud as he left.

They stared at each other in silence—Emma, Hannah and Rachel. Large tears welled up in Hannah's eyes.

Rachel rose to her feet, keeping a protective arm around Hannah's shoulders. "How can he separate the two of them?"

"He can—and it looks like he will," said Emma. "I'm sure he feels that what he does is for the best. After all, he is her grandfather."

"But by bringing charges against Stuart?" Rachel's voice trembled with anger.

Emma eyed her sternly. "Think before you say such things in front of Hannah."

Rachel drew in two deep, shaky breaths, then let them out slowly.

"Some good has come of all this, Rachel. We have to believe things will be better for Hannah now. She'll get the best of care. She'll want for nothing."

Chapter Twenty-Three

Stuart watched without interest as a brown beetle scuttled along the base of the wall toward the bowl of oatmeal mush Sheriff Thorne had placed in his cell that morning. The cereal remained untouched, cold and congealed. A knot the size of a masthead bend had tightened his stomach beyond the point of digestion ever since Dorian had arrived in town yesterday.

Dorian. So changed now since Linnea's death. He tried to conjure up Linnea's image, but found he could no longer recall the distinct lines of her face. When he thought he had them, they shifted in his mind until all he could see was Rachel.

The sound of a carriage pulling to a stop in front of the jail stopped his ruminations. He stood and looked through the window to see Dorian alight, then turn and assist Rachel and Hannah from the transport. Hannah was dressed in traveling clothes, topped with a deep burgundy wool cape and stylish hat to match that must have been purchased by Dorian. She clasped Rachel's hand tightly. Rachel gave Hannah a reassuring smile before walking with her into the building. His heart ached at the sight of them both together—most likely it would be his last.

Sheriff Thorne opened the door and ushered the small group into the room. They remained quiet, unwilling to begin the course that would eventually separate all of them. Even Dorian hung back.

"I…ah…thought you might like a moment alone with the girl," Sheriff Thorne said as he moved to the cell bars and fiddled with the keys to open the lock.

"Just a moment," Dorian suddenly said. "I'd like to talk to Matthew."

The sheriff paused and then nodded.

Rachel raised her brows at Stuart, but clasped Hannah's hand again and said, "We'll just wait in the other room."

Dorian's gaze followed them until the door closed, and then he turned to face Stuart. "I've had the opportunity to learn a few things since speaking with you yesterday."

Stuart remained silent. The man could have his say. It would change little between them.

"I found out that Rachel is more than just a teacher to Hannah, that she has worked miracles with the girl. Truthfully, I am amazed that a stranger would take such an interest in a mute child."

"Rachel has more compassion than most. She told me once that she felt compelled to help Hannah."

"Yes," Dorian said. "I find her quite charming, when I can get past her fierce loyalty to you."

Stuart met his gaze without flinching.

"I heard what she did."

Stuart raised his eyebrows.

"Though I must say people are closemouthed in this small town. The owner of the mercantile was more than willing to give out information. Why Miss Houston cares for you, I cannot fathom, but you've always had a way with the ladies. In any case, she must not realize the whole story." He twisted his hand upon the ivory head of his cane. "Quite noble of you to honor Linnea's memory that way. I thank you for that."

"I loved her."

Under Stuart's steady gaze, it was Dorian who first looked aside. The older man sighed, sat on the bench by the wall and stared through the bars.

"I'm not doing this just for myself, Matthew, just to be cruel. Rose needs that girl. She hasn't been the same since you took Linnea from her. Linnea was the joy of my wife's life and she doesn't know how to let her go. Now Hannah will be that joy. Rose will become whole again."

"I'm sorry, Dorian," Stuart said honestly. He remembered Rose's fragility. "Rose was always good to me."

Nonplussed for a moment Dorian sputtered, "Yes... well." He drew himself up from the seat and cleared his throat. "I came here with the intention of offering you a way out. Against my better judgment, but in respect to the associate you once were to me, I extend it now."

Stuart silently gazed at Dorian, afraid to hope. Whatever his proposal, it would probably cost him dearly.

Dorian cleared his throat. "My bargain is this. You

may have your freedom. I'll drop all charges against you. You will be free to pursue your relationship with your lovely Rachel."

"What do you get out of this?"

"In return, you must give Hannah over to me willingly so that in the future there will be no more battles between us. It will simplify things for me, keeping this out of court, avoiding lawyers."

"What about the murder charge?"

"Like you said. I can call up a few favors and have that taken care of. Although the newspapers pushed the idea that you and Linnea were having an affair and that John had the right to come after you with a gun, I believe you were acting in Linnea's defense. Besides, Rose will not be able to withstand a court battle. She still has a soft spot in her heart for you."

Stuart grasped the bars tightly. "And so you wish me to choose between Rachel and Hannah? Between honoring my vow to Linnea or dishonoring her memory? What kind of choice is that?"

The man's eyebrows rose as he answered smoothly. "A good one, I should think. At least you will have one of them—and your freedom, too."

"You are asking me to break my promise to Linnea. I could never do that."

Dorian sighed and twisted the cane once more, slowly. "I thought that might be the way of it. Although, I had hoped you would come to your senses." He walked to the door. "Say your goodbyes."

The door swung open, and Rachel, Hannah and the sheriff entered. The sheriff fumbled with the key set, finally producing the one that fit the cell lock and opened the door.

"I don't guess you're any danger to these people if I let you see them without bars separating you," Sheriff Thorne said, meeting Stuart's eyes.

"Thank you," Stuart said, understanding the unspoken words and the measure of trust the sheriff granted him.

Hannah burst into the small cell, her face crumpling into tears, her fingers flying as she signed over and over, "Don't make me go. I love you, Daddy."

Stuart lifted her in his arms and hugged her to him, eyes closed, breathing deeply of her soapy scent. He held her tight, unwilling to have this last goodbye end.

Dorian cleared his throat from across the room.

Stuart slowly put Hannah down, but still she clung to him, gripping him fiercely about the waist.

"I must make my ship by this evening. We'll go out with the morning tide," Dorian said. He extended his hand and tapped his cane impatiently on the wooden floor. "Hannah, it's time to leave."

"Give me a minute, won't you?" Stuart glared at him.

Sheriff Thorne stepped forward. "Enough, Taylor."

"Don't you see? He's taking everything! Everything!" Stuart said through gritted teeth. He knelt down at Hannah's level and hugged her once more quickly. "Mind your grandmother Rose. She is a good woman." He looked up at Dorian, unable to keep the anger from his eyes, and then looked back at Hannah. "Write when you can. I'll answer your letters. Rose will give you my address."

Hannah signed, "I want to stay with you."

Stuart shook his head, his heart heavy in his chest. "Your grandparents will take good care of you."

Hannah signed something emphatically and stamped her foot. With that, Dorian gripped Hannah's hand firmly and pulled her tripping toward the door. She struggled against his iron grasp.

"You're hurting her!" Stuart yelled and rushed to the open cell door. Before he could reach Hannah, the sheriff slammed shut the bars. Stuart moved to the window as Dorian dragged Hannah into the carriage and spoke to the driver. Then Dorian turned back and entered the jail.

"Don't ever give her false hope like that. She will not receive any letters."

"It's your call, isn't it? It's always been your call." He grasped the iron bars and jerked them in impotent rage. How much more must he endure?

Dorian nodded smartly to the sheriff, whirled on his heel and walked out of the building.

Rachel leaned against the bars that separated them. Tears glistened in her eyes. "We are going to the light-house to gather Hannah's things and the puppy. Is there anything I can bring back for you?"

He thought about the few items in the house he could call his. "There's a leather satchel under my bed that has a few papers."

"That's it?"

"I never did keep much, remember?" But he was thinking of Linnea, Hannah and Rachel—not things.

"Yes. I remember," she answered softly and turned to leave.

He moved to the window to watch her climb into the carriage. More than anything, he wanted to call her back. How could he stand going on without her? Life without her—without Hannah—would be meaningless. But asking her to stay wouldn't change anything. In the end, it would hurt her more. When he boarded that coach bound for San Francisco and his monkey court, the best thing he could do for Rachel would be to be out of her life for good.

Chapter Twenty-Four

Hannah couldn't believe the tall old man sitting next to her had taken her away from her father. She hated him. He wanted her to teach him some of the hand words but she never would. Not ever. They were special words, just for Father and Rachel and Caleb. She slumped lower in the seat, hoping to get so small that he couldn't see her.

She had heard him say that they would go to his house and it would be a long trip. She always wanted to go on a trip. But not far away, not without her father or Rachel.

She looked out the window of the carriage. They were nearing the lighthouse. Rachel had said she must say goodbye to her house today. She would bring everything with her—her mother's special blanket and the toys in her room, her treasure box of seashells. Grandfather had said he would buy her all new toys once they reached his house. But she didn't want new toys.

The carriage stopped and her grandfather stepped out, turning to help her jump down to the ground. She waited as he placed his funny tall hat on his head and tapped his cane once on the dirt. "Gather your things quickly, my dear," he said. "We need to make haste in order to get to the ship before sundown."

She hated it when he called her dear. She wasn't his dear. She did not even like him—him and his big nose with hair in it. She slowed down, trying to tug her hand from his. She couldn't go on a ship. Didn't he know that? People died on ships! Mother died on one. Her heart started racing in her chest. She tugged harder to free her hand.

Grandfather let go and turned to help Rachel down from the carriage. Hannah raced up to the house and flung open the door looking for Caleb. Where was he? Up the stairs she ran, peeking in each room and cubby-hole until she reached the ladder to the catwalk. She raced back downstairs, past Grandfather and Rachel and out to the shed. Tugging at the heavy door, she finally opened it wide enough to squeeze through. Caleb wasn't there and neither was her puppy. Her heart beat even faster.

"Perhaps they've gone down to the beach, Hannah," said Rachel from the doorway. "I saw some tracks."

Grandfather frowned. "Will they be back soon?"

"I don't know. But Caleb will want to say goodbye to Hannah."

"The climb back up is too steep for me. Leave Hannah here and you go. Be quick about it."

Hannah saw Rachel nod and walk from the shed. She ran after her. She didn't want to be alone with the strange man. His stick came up and blocked her path.

"You and I shall go upstairs and collect your things, young lady."

* * *

"Matthew!" Dorian bellowed. "You manipulated this, didn't you?"

Stuart looked up to see Dorian stride into the sheriff's office and smack his cane on the desk. He walked straight to the door and pulled on the handle. The door was secure. He brandished his cane like a cudgel, waving it erratically. "Sheriff, open this door immediately!"

Thorne ambled over to Dorian. "What's the problem? And what the heck are you doing back here?"

"That's none of your business!" Dorian's voice rose a notch in volume.

"Well, I don't know that you are in a state of mind to see the fellow on the other side of that door."

Stuart gripped the bars of his cell. He'd never seen Dorian so angry—so furiously angry. The man was known for his cool head and unemotional handling of problems.

"What's happened? Is Hannah all right?" Stuart called through the door.

"I'm sure you know better than me," Dorian sputtered. "Now, Sheriff, *open this door!*"

"I'll take your gun again," Sheriff Thorne said calmly.

Dorian dug in his coat pocket and then tossed the derringer to the sheriff.

Thorne unlocked the door, swinging it wide.

"She's gone and well you know it," Dorian said, waving his cane again as he entered the cell room. "You planned this! Anything to see me look a fool."

"Hannah's gone?" Stuart gripped the bars tighter as fear took hold of him. "Where? Dorian. Where?"

"At the lighthouse. She rushed after Rachel, down to the beach to look for Caleb. Well, Caleb came back but not Hannah or Rachel. He never saw them."

Stuart's heart nearly stopped.

Dorian pointed a bony finger at Stuart. "You put the idea into her head. Don't even think about trying to deny it."

Stuart shook his head. "Have you searched everywhere?"

"Caleb went down to look on the beach. It was too steep of a climb for me. I came back here to make sure they hadn't returned here."

Panic knifed through Stuart. "Let me out! Let me find them!"

"Oh, you'd like that, wouldn't you? Do you truly think I could be so gullible?" The ghost of a sickly smile played about his thin lips. "Come, Matthew, you know me better than that."

"She's probably terrified. How could you let her get away from you?" Stuart demanded, his anger matching Dorian's. "She's just a little girl."

"Considering that you planned the whole thing, to her possible detriment I might add, I'm sure you know where she is right now. Safe and cozy."

"You fool! Can't I make you understand that I had nothing to do with this?"

Dorian shook his head. "I'll never believe you, Matthew. This would be the easiest way for you to obtain what you want."

Stuart felt numb inside. With an edge of steel to his voice, he said, "I would never put Hannah at that kind of risk. I would do anything to protect her—even to go so far as handing her over to you."

"Which you did. Remember that. She is mine now."

Stuart shook his head. "You couldn't even protect her for a few hours and yet you blame me for being unable to save Linnea during one of the worst storms at sea in twenty-five years." He pushed his head against the bars and closed his eyes in frustration. There had to be some way to make Dorian see reason. Hannah's life depended on it. "Dorian, please. Let me help. I have to know she is safe. I'll go crazy in here not knowing, not doing something."

For the first time, doubt rose in Dorian's eyes. He stepped backward and sat heavily on the bench along the wall.

Stuart tried to shake the bars. "It will be dark within the hour. We've got to move now!"

Dorian looked vacantly at the sheriff who watched from the doorway and then back at Stuart. "I'll never find her. Not if she doesn't want to be found. And she can move a lot faster than me."

"Your best bet was to get Caleb to help with the search. Hannah trusts him. But I'm your next choice. And I know the area even better."

Dorian sat still as if he hadn't heard.

"You're wasting time you don't have. She may be in trouble. For all we know, she could be hurt and unable to call for help."

Slowly Dorian lifted his gaze to meet Stuart's. "If she would come at the sound of their voices, how much more she would come if you called for her," he said, resignation clearing the furrow between his brows.

Stuart stilled. His heart pounded in his chest as he waited, hoping, yet afraid to hope.

The sheriff stepped closer. "What is it exactly you are saying, Mr. Lansing?"

Dorian paused, staring at Stuart, then said with a sharp edge to his voice, "What I'm saying is, may I have this man released in order to locate my granddaughter?"

"Are you dropping the charges?" the sheriff asked.

Dorian looked sharply at Stuart. "I can't do that. The authorities are waiting in San Francisco to question him regarding a suspicious death. When Hannah is found, she comes with me. The charges stand."

"Well, looks like you're stuck between the bark and the tree, Mr. Taylor. But I expect you to be cooperative," Sheriff Thorne said. "Otherwise, you'll be right back in here and we'll search for the girl without you. Understood?"

Stuart set his jaw. He didn't have a choice. Making sure Hannah and Rachel were safe was all that mattered. He nodded his agreement.

Thorne retrieved the keys from the hook on the wall and unlocked the cell door. "I'll be keeping an eye on you, Taylor."

When Stuart stepped out and came face-to-face with Dorian, he paused, battling with himself to keep from ramming his fist into the man's face.

Dorian kept his eyes on Stuart, acknowledging Stuart's anger. "My carriage is outside."

Chapter Twenty-Five

The sun sank below the horizon, yet its last rays still managed to cast an orange glow over the water and the cliffs. The steady roar of the ocean waves muted everything. Rachel rubbed her throat. She'd called for Caleb until she was hoarse. She'd checked the boat tie-down. Everything looked in order, but Hannah was nowhere to be found.

Down the beach a flutter of yellow among a sandy bed of kelp caught her eye.

Hannah's hair ribbon? Edging closer to the spot, she noticed small footprints in the sand. Then a wave rushed to shore and obliterated the evidence, pushing the strangle of kelp farther up the beach.

Rachel ran down the beach, a premonition building inside.

A puppy barked. It sounded far away. So far that Rachel couldn't be sure she heard it at all.

She picked up her pace and then stopped suddenly, staring in apprehension at the waves licking her feet.

The tide was coming in! Panic rose swift and sharp within her.

Ahead, she heard again a puppy's high-pitched whine blend in with the sounds of the sea.

"Caleb!" she called again. She sloshed through the surf, around the large rock that jutted out into the ocean where they'd hunted at the tidal pools so many months before. The water churned and spit froth as if it were angry, now covering the boulders and rocks that provided a haven for sea creatures. She gave up any hope of keeping her skirt dry as the surf battered her at hip level.

Once to the other side of the rock, she realized that the beach was gone. No one was there—not even a puppy. Had she been wrong to come here? Had she only imagined the puppy's whining? Then she spied the small opening in the cliff wall.

The cavern!

She ducked through the narrow opening, stumbling at the dip in the sandy floor, and then straightened inside a small alcove. Water swirled around her knees here, but a few more steps and she reached dry sand. Although, she knew it wouldn't be dry for long. The last rays of the setting sun made the cavern walls glow orange.

In the dim light, Hannah crouched in a niche, the puppy playfully out of reach in front of her.

"Hannah!" Rachel could barely believe her own eyes.

Hannah spun around. Her dress was dirty and wrinkled, her hair tangled and stringy, but otherwise she looked fine.

Then Rachel noticed that her cheeks were wet with tears.

Rachel ran to her and enveloped her, shivering, into her arms. The puppy dashed up and yipped at them, and then danced just beyond their reach.

"Having trouble catching him?" She wiped Hannah's face. "I'll help."

They approached the animal from opposite sides. Yet, over and over the pup dashed between their outstretched hands. Rachel quickly became frustrated.

"This isn't working, Hannah. And we have to go. The tide is getting too high to wait any longer."

She peeled off her cloak. The next time the puppy made its wild dash, Rachel threw the cloak as though she was casting for fish. The heavy wool material landed on the puppy, stopping it just long enough for Rachel to grab it and bundle it up.

"Let's get to your house before the ti—" Her voice faltered as she glanced at the narrow opening. The surf rushed in and it was way over Hannah's head. They had to get out—now.

She met and held Hannah's gaze, then purposely squatted and released the puppy. Hannah started to run past her to capture the pet, but Rachel grabbed her shoulders and forced her to meet her gaze.

"If there is time, I'll come back for the puppy, but right now you are the most important thing. You must get out of here. The pup will be scared, but she'll be all right." Rachel hoped she spoke the truth.

Hannah's eyes widened in fright. She tried to sign something, her finger ballet frantic and disjointed.

Finally Rachel made out the word *drown*. Was Hannah thinking about her mother? Remembering? "Come here, honey." Rachel caught her to her, intending only to pick her up, but the embrace for reassurance ended in a fierce hug. She took a deep breath and looked into worried eyes. "Grab on to me. Tight."

Hannah flung her arms around Rachel's neck. "Now, don't let go for anything."

The water pounded against her, twisting and tugging her heavy skirt, trying to knock her down. The ground was uneven, and where the floor of the cave dipped, the water rose to her waist.

At the entrance, the force of the surf increased, buffeting them about, the icy spray drenching them both. The water plastered her hair to her face, blinding her to the small amount of graying twilight. The ocean roared about them, swirling and crashing. A wave thundered over them and forced them under. They surfaced, sputtering and spitting the saltwater from their mouths.

Frantically Rachel tried to regain her footing. A person could be washed out to sea. She'd heard it said that even strong sailors were no match for the tides if the ocean had a mind to take them. She struggled to keep Hannah's head above water while the girl clung to her side and the water pulled at her skirt and legs. Stuart had already lost one he loved to the sea. Rachel refused to let the sea have another.

Suddenly her feet found the uneven sandy bottom. She braced herself for an instant, unsure of her footing, when another wave crashed through the small inlet and shoved them back into the cavern.

"The water's too strong," she said in gasps. *And cold.* Her lips must be blue, they were so numb.

In the last of the dim light, the distinct features of Hannah's face faded into a blur of grayness. Rachel clung to her, shivering and listening to the roar of each wave barreling toward them, wondering if this would be the wave, larger than the rest, that would cover them.

"It's almost too dark to see anything," Sheriff Thorne said as they approached the lighthouse. "Even the lanterns aren't much help. We ought to start in the morning."

"No!" thundered Stuart and Dorian simultaneously.

"I won't stop," said Stuart. "Not for a minute."

The sheriff took off his Stetson and wiped his brow. "Look, Taylor. They could be anywhere."

"I'm not quitting!" Stuart growled. "I know this peninsula better than either of you."

The beam from the lighthouse flashed over them for the first time that night. Caleb was in the tower.

Stuart grabbed a lantern and rope from the shed, and then searched the area for signs of Hannah. He found the tracks of her small-size brogans heading toward the beach trail. "Don't expect me back for several hours. Sheriff, you're welcome to follow if you think I'll escape." He headed down the trail at a run, the sheriff somewhere behind him.

Skidding and sliding, he raced as though the devil chased him, apprehension building. Ignoring the switchbacks and the trail, he raced straight down, grabbing at sage and brush for balance. Often he had nothing to steady himself but the dirt, where broken shells bloodied his hands. He dropped the glowing lantern at the last bit of even ground and then slid the last ten feet to the bottom at such a speed that he couldn't stop and splashed into the ocean. He gasped as the icy water closed around his waist. The tide was on its way in. Soon there'd be no safe place along this part of the beach.

He waded farther into the water, pushing through with a sense of vengeance. Waves crashed into him, determined to thrust him against the jagged cliff formations. He slipped once and scraped up against the sandstone, then braced himself and pushed steadily onward, ignoring the sting of the saltwater in his eyes and on the raw scrapes of his hands.

There was only one place they could be if they were still on the beach. Otherwise they would have made it to higher ground and back to the lighthouse by now.

The cave.

The large fishing rock loomed dark and forbidding before him. It jutted out into the water just far enough to make going around difficult, and with its sides too sheer to climb from this position. If…*if*…he made it around without drowning himself, he wasn't sure he could make it back. But he had to know that Rachel and Hannah were not trapped on the other side. He had to…

Stumbling over rocks and boulders in his path, Stuart fought as the water pushed and pulled him relentlessly. In some small recess of his brain he noted the temperature was frigid and the feeling in his fingers had gone beyond numb. They were not responding like they should.

Finally he rounded the large rock that partially hid the inlet to the small cave. It was too dark to see the cave now, but he knew well enough it was there—somewhere ahead of him.

"Rachel!" he called over the roar of the waves. "Rachel!"

"I'm here!"

His heart lodged in his throat. He'd found her. The current pulled against him, trying to drag him out to sea. He struggled and pushed ahead. Then a wave found his back and the force of the water hurtled him toward the narrowed inlet. At least, he hoped that was where he was heading since he couldn't see much. Suddenly his face scraped against the gritty sand floor. He pushed up and struggled to stand, the water just above his waist.

The sound was different here. The roar of the ocean muffled.

He was inside the cave.

Breathing heavily, he wiped the water off his face. He could barely discern someone's shape just ahead of him. He started toward the figure when small hands gripped his arm.

"My God!" He felt the straggly hair on the head before him. "Hannah!" He whisked her into his arms and hugged her, rubbing her hair, her face, her shoulders. "Are you all right?"

In the crook between his cheek and shoulder, he felt her nod, then shiver. Relief washed through him. "Rachel?"

"I'm fine." Her voice came from a few feet away, trembling. "We tried to get out but the water was too strong." Slowly the curve of her shoulders became visible. A swift need to touch her overwhelmed him. He had to reassure himself that she, too, was all right, that she was real. He reached for her, drawing her firmly against his wet chest. She melted against him, sliding her arm around his waist.

"Thank God you're here, Stuart."

He crushed his lips to hers, drawing what warmth he could from her lips, and in turn trying to infuse her with a portion of his strength. Perhaps God had had a hand in this.

"How did you know where to look for us?" Her teeth chattered from the cold.

"Gut instinct." He pulled her close again, unwilling to let her go. "We have to get out of here."

"But…are you free now?"

"Not exactly."

He could barely see the outline of the cave opening. A few stars twinkled in the night sky just beyond it. As he judged his options, a cold fist closed over his heart while the awful truth dawned.

"What is it?" Rachel asked.

The irony of the situation seeped through him, forcing a single bitter laugh. It wasn't enough that he'd lost Linnea and been haunted by her face in his dreams ever since. No—now he must face nearly the same thing again.

"Stuart?" Rachel's voice was rich with concern.

He ran his hand through his hair, pushing the wet

strands back from his forehead, his fingers skimming the edges of the scar—remembering.

"It's not the same," Rachel said. "Not the same situation at all."

He stilled.

"You told me Linnea pushed Hannah at you. If anyone was going to be saved she wanted it to be Hannah. She made the choice."

"You weren't there. You don't know." He hadn't meant to growl out the words, but his frustration doubled by the second. After living with his choice, he didn't need Rachel arguing the point with him. "I can only take one of you at a time—not both."

"But—"

"The surf is too strong," he lashed out at her. "I can't take you both."

He sensed her still beside him. "Then there is no choice at all."

He wished he could see her face better, but it was too dark. Her face had always told him what she thought. "I won't go until I'm sure you understand. I must take Hannah first. I can't leave her in here."

"Of course you can't. She's frightened enough as it is. I'll just wait for you."

Her calm reply almost undid him. He had asked so much of her, and still she seemed to trust him. He brushed his fingers down her soft cheek and felt her chin tremble. "I'll be back as soon as Hannah is on high ground," he murmured.

"I know."

He took a deep breath, then turned to Hannah.

"We're going for a swim, short stuff," he said with a confidence he did not feel. "This may be a little wild, so whatever happens don't let go of me. And I won't let go of you."

She grasped his neck as he waded back into the water. The urge to look back once at Rachel was strong, but he resisted, refusing to have another memory etched in his mind that might stay with him forever. *I'll just wait for you,* she'd said. He'd be back, he vowed silently.

He made his way toward the opening until the water came to his chest. Together, he and Hannah braced as the first wave thundered toward them. He shouted in her ear, and at the last minute, rather than fight the current, they ducked under the water, allowing the wave to churn violently above their heads. When they resurfaced, Hannah coughed and spit water, and they could see the stars overhead.

They were out of the cave.

He let the outgoing water carry them until he sensed they were heading beyond the rock and then he struggled to get out of its grasp. He forced his way through the surf, rounding the jagged rock, and then let an incoming wave carry them toward the cliff. Three more waves propelled them farther. Holding Hannah's hand firmly in his, Stuart and she finally arrived at the base of the trail, both out of breath, but both very much safe.

"Now, Hannah. I want you to crawl up the trail and wait for me by the lantern. I'm going back for Rachel."

She nodded, shivering, and he hugged her tight.

"If…" He hated to say it. He took a deep breath. "If

I don't come back, you must climb up the trail to the lighthouse. Caleb is there. Do you understand?"

Again she nodded, and he hugged her tight. "I love you, short stuff."

A brave smile worked its way past the shivers.

He turned back into the surf.

When he entered the small cavern again, he could no longer see—not even an outline. And the water was up to his thighs on the highest ground. "Rachel?"

A puppy whined.

"Rachel?"

"I'm all right, Stuart. I'm here."

"Ready?"

"Can you manage the pup, too?"

He hesitated.

"I could tie him up with a strip of my petticoat."

He thought for a moment. "Keep hold of the dog." He reached his hand around her waist and drew her close, flattening her against him. "The skirt will have to go. It will drag you down." With that, he unbuttoned the waistband and pushed the skirt down below the water. "Step out."

When she'd done so, he grabbed the hem of her petticoat and ripped a strip of cloth, then tied it around the dog's middle.

"Ready?"

"Yes," she said breathlessly.

His mouth found hers in the dark. He tightened his arms around her and kissed her thoroughly. Her lips were smooth and immeasurably giving. "I love you, Rachel Houston."

"I know, Stuart." She smiled against his mouth, and he felt her shiver.

"Don't let go."

"Never."

The tide rose with every minute they delayed. He took her hand and they waded toward the sound of waves crashing against the cliff. He gripped her hand tighter. "Now!"

They surged forward with the water as it receded from the cave. Another, larger wave battered them, tugging at them, trying to separate them. Stuart held on tight. He would not lose Rachel. Not this way. He strained to see in the inky blackness. If only he could see the waves coming, he'd be able to anticipate and dive under them.

Another wave washed over their heads. He came up choking and sputtering, pulling Rachel up, up, to where she could get air. He heard her gasp beside him.

Then they were out in the starlight. He felt for the sheer face of the fishing rock. The water was over his head, now, but as long as he stayed near the rock, they would make it.

They endured the brutal crash of the water over them once more, and though his fingers were raw from gripping the jagged edge, he still managed to shield Rachel from much of the force of the wave.

Finally they were around the rock and headed toward the cliff and the trail.

They came to the spot that Stuart had left Hannah, and Stuart sat down, hands on his knees, and dragged in several deep breaths. Rachel, next to him, did the same. A shiver racked her body.

"We have to get warm," he said gruffly, looking around for Hannah, realizing suddenly that a second lantern glowed nearby. Hannah stood in its glow, next to the sheriff.

"I'll help the girl," Sheriff Thorne said, lifting his lantern to take a good look at each of them. "And I'll hang on to that pup, too."

Stuart handed him the end of cloth that secured the dog. A hot fire sounded better than anything right now. He reached for Rachel, and she grasped his hand.

On the trek to the lighthouse, he never let go.

Chapter Twenty-Six

When they entered the lighthouse, Dorian looked up from his seat in front of the small fire. He looked ten years older.

"You found her. Thank God. Caleb, bring some blankets."

Caleb looked to Stuart.

"In the chest at the foot of the stairs." Stuart walked over to the fire and shoveled more coal pellets into it.

Dorian wrapped Hannah in the first quilt. He sat in the rocker by the fire and pulled her onto his lap.

Stuart watched them for a moment, surprised that Hannah had allowed herself to be held by Dorian, but even more surprised at Dorian's demeanor. Gone was the commanding authoritarian, replaced by a gentle man whose only concern was Hannah's well-being.

"Her trunk is in the kitchen," Rachel said. "I'll get some dry clothes."

Stuart followed her into the room. "Thank you for being there," he said, tugging the blanket closer around her shoulders. She looked so bedraggled, that he gave up any pretense and, using the blanket, pulled her against him. He kissed her gently. "Thank God you're safe," he murmured against her lips. "I love you, Rachel."

"I never thought to hear you say those words," she said softly, "and now you said them twice in one evening."

"I should have told you long ago."

A small smile tilted her lips. "What will happen now? Will you have to go back to jail?"

"I don't know. Dorian holds the cards."

They stood embracing, cold and shivering, both reluctant to let go.

Sheriff Thorne cleared his throat by the doorway. "I realize you're creating your own heat there, but I think the two of you better get by the fire or you'll both catch cold."

Caleb watched from behind the sheriff. Stuart suppressed a smile as he felt Rachel stiffen slightly when she noticed him.

"Would you put on some water for tea, Caleb? And might I borrow some dry clothes?" Rachel asked in a high voice. At his nod, she moved out of Stuart's arms and headed up the stairs. She paused on the bottom step as the sheriff spoke.

"I'll be heading back to town just as soon as everyone's warmed up, Miss Houston."

She looked at Stuart, but her answer was for the sheriff. "I'll be ready."

Stuart found a nightgown for Hannah in the trunk.

Hannah was in such an exhausted state that she only grumbled slightly as he changed her into the dry gown, then she snuggled back onto her grandfather. He took a seat by the fire with Dorian, noting that the sheriff had pulled in a chair from the kitchen to join them. "So," he said after a long silence, "where do we go from here?"

Dorian sighed. "This whole business doesn't sit well with me." He brushed a wisp of hair off Hannah's cheek.

Gone was the strong, strident voice, the confidence that Stuart had come to expect from Dorian. There was a hesitation totally foreign to his usual manners.

"I've had a lot of time to think, along with my worrying about Hannah's safety, while you were trying to find her. I…I don't feel right having things end this way. I've come to some conclusions about you…about me and Rose. At one time I thought replacing the daughter we lost with our granddaughter would make things right again."

Stuart wondered where this would lead, afraid to let himself hope.

"I was wrong."

Dorian stared at the fire through watery eyes. "It has been hard on all of us to lose Linnea."

Stuart stopped breathing. Had Dorian just said "us"? As in, including him?

"She was my world. But now, to nearly lose Hannah…" His voice trailed off for a moment. "Well, I place the blame entirely on my own shoulders."

Stuart had never seen Dorian so shattered.

"These past few years have changed all of us, but at one time you were as near to a son as could be to me. I don't think you've changed all that much." He grimaced. "Maybe I'm the one who changed—or didn't change when I should have."

He shifted in the rocker to look at Stuart. "You may be unaware that the banker, Mr. Furst, was prepared to cover the cost of my missing cargo along with any legal fees you incurred. He said you refused any reward for saving his son."

Stuart nodded carefully, afraid to break the course of Dorian's thoughts.

"Guess you've made a few powerful friends of your own. Well, the Fursts can keep their money. That isn't what this was about and you and I both know it. The lost cargo was just a means to finding you—a means to an end. And that end isn't anything I anticipated."

He stopped rocking and looked down. Hannah was fast asleep in his arms.

"I'll put her to bed, sir," Caleb said. At the older man's nod, Caleb gathered Hannah up and took her up the stairs. Stuart listened as the boy's footsteps sounded overhead in Hannah's bedroom.

Dorian met Stuart's gaze. "The enquiry into the death of Linnea's husband will just be a formality. I'll bear witness to the fact that he abused her and she was frightened for her life and the life of their daughter. Linnea killed him, Stuart. Not you, as much as you may have believed that. The doctor's autopsy showed it was the bullet from her gun—the gun I'd given her on her twentieth birthday—that lodged in his spleen. It took him a while to die and so he followed her straight to you."

Dazed at this new information, Stuart murmured, "But I shot him…."

"Your bullets struck his hip and shoulder. They made him fall, too weak from loss of blood to get back up."

A huge weight lifted from Stuart's shoulders. "All this time, I thought I'd killed him."

Dorian smiled sadly. "I taught my daughter to protect herself. She certainly did."

Stuart tried to take in all that Dorian had said. After so many years of believing he'd murdered John Newcomb, to learn the truth took a bit of reckoning.

"Because of Newcomb's notoriety, the newspapers had a field day, sensationalizing your link to Linnea. And I chose to believe them over you."

"I loved your daughter, sir."

"I know that now. And I know you would have done everything in your power to save her that night at sea."

"I tried. I wanted the sea to take me, not her."

"Yes, I understand that now. I've been foolish. And stubborn." Dorian stood and walked the few steps to lean his hand against the fireplace mantel and stared into the fire. "You really were the better man for her, Matthew. If only things had worked out differently."

Stuart swallowed hard. To have Dorian admit so much left him stunned. Slowly his thoughts returned to the present, and his promise to Linnea. "So where does that leave us, Dorian? Do you still plan to take Hannah to San Francisco?"

The quiet that followed his question was deafening. Only the crackling of the fire could be heard.

Dorian turned to face him. "Yes, I do."

Stuart dropped his head into his hands. He'd hoped—he didn't know what he'd hoped. There was no way, having found Hannah, Dorian would let her go again. He tried to focus on what Dorian was saying.

"And you need to come back, too. You must clear up this business of Newcomb. Perhaps while there, we can have Hannah see a specialist regarding her voice."

"What about Hannah's father's relatives? Will they cause any trouble?"

"I guess we'll face that if it comes. We'll face it together."

Emotion overcame Stuart. This was not the man he'd left three years ago. Strange to have their paths bring them back full circle.

"You are welcome in our home. Rose has asked for you a number of times over the past year. It would do her heart good to see you."

"Thank you, Dorian." He could barely get the words out.

"Pack your things while you're upstairs."

Stuart stood, for the first time noticing that Rachel had come back dressed in Caleb's old trousers. She listened from the doorway, an unreadable expression on her face.

He was going to leave her. Rachel leaned against the door frame for support. She had hoped, with all that had gone between them this night, that he would be able to stay. That he would want to stay.

He grabbed her hand and pulled her into the kitchen. "I have to do this, Rachel. This is my chance."

She nodded but couldn't meet his gaze.

"I've got to clear my name. You understand that, don't you?"

She was numb inside. That's all she understood. "You don't need to explain anything to me."

"Yes, I do. I know you don't want me to leave. If I don't go to San Francisco and take care of this, I'll always wonder if someone is out there looking for me—Linnea's husband's family or a trigger-happy bounty hunter."

Her heart was being cut in two. She could feel the chasm, the pain in her chest. In that moment she could almost hate him. Almost but not quite. Because try as she might to feel nothing, she still loved him. On some small level deep inside, she did know why he had to leave.

"I really do understand, Stuart. Now go upstairs and take care of your things. I'm sure Mr. Lansing will want to leave as quickly as possible."

He took hold of her shoulders, forcing her to turn toward him, acknowledge him. "Please look at me, Rachel."

Slowly her eyes met his.

"I don't know how this will turn out. I can't promise you anything. I have to take one day at a time."

"Believe me, I don't expect anything," she said bitterly.

He shook her gently. "I'm not just one more person leaving you," he said earnestly.

Her chin notched up. "No. You are two more people leaving. But you know something? It's okay. I've got a lot to do over the next few months—the teaching examination, getting my job back. You don't figure into any of that."

He frowned and stepped back, lowering his hands.

She knew she was pushing him away, but he didn't realize how he was hurting her. "You better go get your things together, Stuart. Daylight will come soon enough and I imagine Mr. Lansing will want to leave on the morning tide as he has planned."

He nodded slowly. "Rachel—"

"I…I don't know if I will make it to the dock in the morning. Give my love to Hannah and tell her to write."

"She'll write, and so will I." He started toward her.

"Stuart, please," she suddenly begged, her voice breaking. "Don't make this any harder for me." She turned away from him, blindly swiping at the tears in her eyes. Stepping into the parlor, she spied the one she needed. "Sheriff? Could you take me home now?"

"From the look on your face, I'd say you missed the sea," Dorian said, his gaze more than a little sly. "At least from this vantage point."

"Some," Stuart admitted, enjoying the roll of the steamer's deck beneath his feet. "More than I realized."

He circled his arm around Hannah's shoulders. Having him with her had lessened her fear of the ship, and Stuart found that daylight also eased her fears. He looked from her blond head down into the kelp beds that floated beside the ship. Linnea's vision no longer haunted him, nor the guilt he had carried for so long. Although he couldn't be sure how he would fare until the court hearing was over, for the first time in years he felt free.

"I'm not sure I approve of my granddaughter learning some of the words my crew members use," Dorian said. "She will certainly raise her grandmother's eyebrows if Rose catches on to her hand signals."

Stuart chuckled. "Rose will just have to take her for what she is."

"It could become her goal in life to smooth the rough edges you've given the girl."

"Hannah will handle it." Besides, after hearing of Rose's declining condition, he suspected seeing Hannah would do Rose's heart good. Truth be told, he missed her, too. To see her again would be good for him.

A spark of light on the peninsula caught his eye. Although it was early morning, the lantern at the lighthouse flashed once, twice, three times. Beside him, Hannah stood on her toes and pointed to the light, and then waved wildly.

"Caleb?" Dorian asked.

Stuart nodded.

"Goodbye and good journey," Dorian translated the light's familiar message to sailors. "It would seem you have made a few loyal friends here."

"A few," he murmured, his thoughts on Rachel. He had looked for her on the docks this morning, but she hadn't come to see them off. Just as she'd said. Already she was pushing him away.

He had to do this. He wished he could make her

understand. If he was to ever have a future with her, he had to do this. He only hoped Dorian was right and all charges would be dropped after the investigation.

Chapter Twenty-Seven

One Month Later

Rachel hurried across the street toward the mercantile. Her monthly had come this morning, and with it the cramping. Perhaps the store had a powder to ease the discomfort. She'd half hoped she might be carrying Stuart's baby. How wonderful it would have been to have a small part of him. But the practical part of her knew it would be catastrophic. She would never be able to support a child on her own. She stepped inside.

"Rachel?" Elizabeth called out. "A letter came for you this morning. I was going to run it over to you on my lunch break, but since you're here, let me see if I can find it. Ah, here it is." Elizabeth walked around the end of the counter and handed the envelope to her.

She tore apart the waxed seal, imprinted with a bold M.S.T. and scanned the letter.

Miss Rachel Houston:
Hannah and I arrived safely in San Francisco. It was something to see the look on Rose's face when she first saw her granddaughter. I don't think I ever told you, but Hannah is the image of Linnea.

Additional charges from Newcomb's family have postponed the court date. They are making things more difficult. I'm expecting no leniency from the judge. The jail here is adequate—but I miss Thornton's philosophical discussions—especially since I may be here a long time.

I hope the town there has come to their senses and let you resume teaching their children. They're fools if they don't. Wish things had turned out differently between you and me. Wish a lot of things.
Matthew Stuart Taylor

Rachel's hand shook as she read the message again. Her eyes burned with tears. It didn't sound like he expected to be freed.

A rustling sound from behind made her turn quickly to the spools of thread. The colors swam before her eyes. Numbly, she picked up a spool of blue. She thought she'd toughened up. In the weeks since Stuart had gone, she'd tried hard to put the past behind her and get on with her life.

"Excuse me, Rachel?" Elizabeth said.

"Yes," she answered, unable to look Elizabeth in the eye, her thoughts still focused on Stuart.

"Is it from the Mr. Taylor?"

She nodded numbly.

"How is Hannah? Is she adjusting to San Francisco?"

Rachel blew out a shaky sigh. "He didn't say much, but it sounds like she is."

"Are you all right?"

She nodded quickly, but a sob slipped past her lips. She clasped her hand over her mouth. Her one-time friend hadn't initiated a conversation with her in over two months, and now she picked a fine time to show concern—when Rachel was ready to blubber like a fool. Desperately she struggled to take hold of her emotions.

"You must miss them terribly," Elizabeth said carefully.

Rachel raised her gaze but was unable to focus for the water in her eyes. "They are doing well. That's enough." Of course it wasn't, but she wasn't going to say more to Elizabeth. Some things were too dear to talk about, especially to someone who had shunned her. She squared her shoulders and folded the note, placing it in her reticule. Her actions couldn't have announced more clearly that she was preparing to leave. But Elizabeth seemed oblivious to her signals, or else refused to acknowledge them.

"I hear you passed the teaching exam."

Rachel stopped en route to the door. If Elizabeth, who didn't even have children in the school, was going to give her difficulty about wanting to teach, she'd better think again.

"So even after all that has happened you still want to teach?"

She braced herself, prepared to endure yet another snide comment. "Yes. If I can convince the school board to give me the chance. If not, I'll look elsewhere."

Elizabeth held out a handkerchief. "Then I hope you get your chance."

Caught off guard, Rachel looked at Elizabeth in confusion. When all she saw in the woman's face was honest concern, she slowly relaxed her stance and took the cloth. "Thank you."

Elizabeth smiled tentatively. "You have a gift for teaching. You did wonders with Hannah. You loved them both, didn't you?"

Startled again by the woman's perception, Rachel asked, "It's that obvious?"

"You look that miserable."

Rachel let out a sigh, thinking of Stuart. "But I don't have any regrets, Elizabeth. I'd do it all over again in a heartbeat."

Elizabeth nodded slowly, understanding in her face. "I know."

And Rachel suddenly realized that she did. "How did you learn of the certificate?"

"Terrance mentioned when it arrived in the mail. I, ah, suppose you heard that he's courting Amanda now."

"I heard. They are suited for each other."

Elizabeth's brown eyes took on a mischievous glint. "Oh, Rachel! How can you say that? I cannot imagine her as my sister-in-law. After an hour we are like two pieces of sandpaper."

A smile, the first real one in a long time, tugged at Rachel's lips.

"That's better," Elizabeth said. "Now, what can I help you find?"

Rachel looked blankly at the spool of blue thread in her hand, and then slowly placed it back on the rack. "Shoes," she said, this time with determination. "I need them for my interview with the school board."

Elizabeth tapped her finger against her cheek, deep in thought for a moment. "Then I have a suggestion. Let's go into New San Diego and see the display at Marston's store. We'll see what type of competition Terrance and I are up against to try to bring more business here and we can see the latest in spring fashion."

Rachel found herself smiling at Elizabeth's enthusiasm. And if the town council approved Rachel's position—then she would be able to get on with her life.

She would be a good teacher, she vowed to herself. She would gain the town's respect again. She drew the drawstring tight on her bag, thinking of the letter within. And she would never trust her heart to another man. Obviously, any further pining on her part for what could have been was futile. Stuart had left for good. He wasn't coming back. Ever.

Chapter Twenty-Eight

April 1874

Stuart strode up the main street of La Playa with Hannah tugging relentlessly at his hand, urging him to go faster. His ship had steamed into port just this morning and he'd quickly delegated the duties of unloading Dorian's wares to his first mate. With that task underway, he made his way directly to the parsonage, his thoughts on one auburn-haired woman.

Reverend Crouse answered Stuart's knock. "Taylor! And Hannah too! A surprise indeed!"

"Come in," Emma Crouse said, peering from behind her husband.

Hannah didn't hold back when it came to someone she considered a friend. She rushed in and threw her arms around the woman. A look of delight crossed Emma's face. "It's good to see you again, Hannah. Just look at you! All dressed up like a little sailor."

Stuart removed his hat and tucked it under his arm. "I'm in town for just a few days."

Reverend Crouse eyed Stuart's gold-buttoned frock coat. "So you've gone back to the sea?"

"Yes, sir." He looked about the parlor, expecting Rachel to walk in.

"Well, I hope you'll feel welcome to drop in when you are docked here in La Playa."

Startled at the reverend's warm greeting, Stuart met his gaze. "Thank you. I appreciate that."

Emma Crouse stood up from hugging Hannah. "Would you like to come in for some tea?"

He shook his head. "Thank you, but no. I'd like a word with Rachel—Miss Houston."

"She isn't at here just now," Reverend Crouse answered.

Disappointment set in swiftly. Stuart was ready to turn the town upside down to find her. "Where is she?"

"She won't be home until late afternoon."

Hannah's expression changed from one of excitement to downcast, and the buoyant spirit that had accompanied Stuart the entire voyage faded away. "I see. Then, with your permission, I'll call back later this evening."

"Oh, Stanley, quit drawing this out," Emma said, pinching her husband playfully on his arm.

Reverend Crouse rubbed his chin and studied them both with twinkling eyes. "Rachel would sure hate to miss seeing the two of you. Perhaps you can interrupt her for a moment. She's teaching at the school."

"Teaching?"

"Has been for two months now."

"Then the school board didn't fire her after all?"

Reverend Crouse smiled. "She held her own against those rascals. Convinced them their children would be the losers if they let her go."

Pride for Rachel overwhelmed Stuart. "That's great! And she was right. They're the ones who would have been sorry."

"Now, you make sure and stop back here before you leave port," said Emma. "And bring Hannah."

"Thank you." Stuart backed off the porch. "I'll make sure to stop in and see Caleb later."

"You do that."

He headed up the street with Hannah. Teaching again! A fierce pride swelled in his chest. She hadn't let the town beat her down. What an amazing woman. But then, he'd known that she had grit the minute she refused to back down when she'd wanted to teach Hannah sign language. How many times had they argued over that?

And now she was teaching again...that changed everything! He had thought to swoop in and rescue her from this town of shortsighted fools, but now what? She had made them see things her way—had proved she was worth hiring back.

He would be a complication.

He reached the schoolyard, all his senses on edge. Two dark-haired boys, nine or ten years of age, stood in the shade of the schoolhouse and stared at Hannah, then turned and raced through the open doorway. Bees buzzed around the large gray-green saltbushes to each side of the door.

Rachel's voice drifted out to them. Although her words were muffled, her soft twang enveloped Stuart. He quickened his pace up the walk and stopped within the doorway.

Bedlam greeted him. Children ran about the classroom, jumping from bench to bench. But he didn't care. There was only one person he wanted to see. Where the hell was she?

Suddenly, a paper bird sailed across the air to hit…a very female derriere. The woman picked up the paper from the floor and straightened, stretching out her lower back.

Rachel.

Flushed, disheveled—beautiful. And happy.

"I think you have that aircraft down now, Percy. Why don't you try a different—"

She caught sight of him at the door and froze.

A chalk mark slashed across her jaw. Her dark-auburn hair was knotted messily high on the back of her head with a pencil stabbed into the thick mass, reminding him of all the times her hair had come undone by the wind on the peninsula.

His heart lurched in his chest. She was so beautiful, so full of life. She filled the room with it. He wanted to smile but couldn't. She looked so happy. Would she want him?

He'd rehearsed his lines on the voyage south and now he couldn't think of a thing to say that would be right. At his side, Hannah tugged his sleeve. When he didn't budge, she gave him a puzzled looked, let go of him and ran to Rachel.

Rachel squatted and opened her arms, enclosing Hannah in a warm embrace. A powerful yearning overtook Stuart. A yearning to hold Rachel like that, to feel her against him. She rose and waited.

She wasn't smiling. And she hadn't made a move to come closer. Maybe he'd been away too long. Maybe things had changed more than he thought. He glanced quickly at her left hand. No ring. He exhaled in relief.

Then he realized he was the one to take those last few steps. Even though he'd come five hundred miles for her, he'd also left her in the first place. Just like her father. It was up to him to come back.

All the way.

"Hello, Rachel." He stepped toward her. He should say more, but nothing came to mind. All he could think about was that he was here with her—finally here. And she was standing too far away.

Then it came to him. The one thing she'd driven him crazy with, the one thing they'd argued about. He took a deep breath. "Hannah's going to start school."

Rachel glanced down at the top of Hannah's head. Her gaze came back to his and he saw tears. She sniffed and wiped at her eyes. "Well, it's about time. She never even wrote. One might think she didn't know how."

He swallowed, thinking of the countless letters he'd written and then torn up before sending her. The children were listening with wide eyes—and ears. "I'm back working with shipping. A free man now," he said, stepping closer, breathing in the honeysuckle scent of her. How he'd missed that. "The courts have cleared me."

"That's wonderful, Stuart. You have everything you want now—Hannah, your freedom."

At one time that would have been enough. He'd learned otherwise. He touched her chin, cupped her cheek with his hand. "No, I don't. Not nearly enough. I don't have you."

Her gaze slammed into his. At her side, Hannah's face split into a huge grin. More than a few of the children craned their heads to see around others.

Let them listen. This was too important to worry about what tales they would carry home to their parents. "I'm starting over and I want you by my side. Where we live doesn't matter—here or in San Francisco. You can choose."

She didn't answer. Why didn't she answer? He saw his future fading beyond his reach. "I'm not leaving, Rachel. Do you hear me? I'll never leave again."

"Stuart."

"I love you, Rachel. You know I love you."

She stood still, her gaze on his. Slowly she raised her arms to cross her chest, signing the words back to him.

His heart soared. "Let me hear you say them."

She stepped close and cupped a warm hand over his mouth.

His heart thudded faster in his chest.

She tilted her face up. In her eyes shone a love he'd waited a lifetime to see. "I love you, too, and my answer is yes."

He kissed her palm, then brushed away her hand. He had to kiss her—taste her chin, her cheeks, her mouth. He leaned toward her.

Her eyes widened as she realized his intent. "The children, Stuart…"

A devilish smile worked its way up his face. "This is school, Miss Houston. Let's show them how it's done."

He scooped her off her feet and into his arms, twirling her around in a circle. She let out a breathless shriek of delight. Then, stopping, he lowered his lips to hers…and claimed her and his future in one deep, heart-stirring kiss.

* * * * *

Turn the page for a sneak preview
of the first book in the new miniseries
DIAMONDS DOWN UNDER
from Silhouette Desire®,
VOWS & A VENGEFUL GROOM
by Bronwyn Jameson

Available January 2008

Silhouette Desire®
Always Powerful, Passionate and Provocative

Kimberley Blackstone didn't notice the waiting horde of media until it was too late. Flashbulbs exploded around her like a New Year's light show. She skidded to a halt, so abruptly her trailing suitcase all but overtook her.

This had to be a case of mistaken identity. Surely. Kimberley hadn't been on the paparazzi hit list for close to a decade, not since she'd estranged herself from her billionaire father and his headline-hungry diamond business.

But no, it was *her* name they called. *Her* face was the focus of a swarm of lenses that circled her like avid hornets. Her heart started to pound with fear-fueled adrenaline.

What did they want?

What was going on?

With a rising sense of bewilderment she scanned the crowd for a clue, and her gaze fastened on a tall, leonine figure forcing his way to the front. A tall, familiar figure. Her head came up in stunned recognition, and their gazes collided across the sea of heads before the cameras erupted with another barrage of flashes, this time right in her exposed face.

Blinded by the flashbulbs—and by the shock of that

momentary eye-meet—Kimberley didn't realize his intent until he'd forged his way to her side, possibly by the sheer strength of his personality. She felt his arm wrap around her shoulder, pulling her into the protective shelter of his body, allowing her no time to object. No chance to lift her hands to ward him off.

In the space of a hastily drawn breath, she found herself plastered knee-to-nose against six feet two inches of hard-bodied male.

Ric Perrini.

Her lover for ten torrid weeks, her husband for ten tumultuous days.

Her ex for ten tranquil years.

After all this time, he should not have felt so familiar but, oh dear, he did. She knew the scent of that body and its lean, muscular strength. She knew its heat and its slick power and every response it could draw from hers.

She also recognized the ease with which he'd taken control of the moment and the decisiveness of his deep voice when it rumbled close to her ear. "I have a car waiting outside. Is this your only luggage?"

Kimberley nodded. "I assume you will tell me," she said tightly, "what this welcome party is all about."

"Not while the welcome party is within earshot. No."

Barking a request for the cameramen to stand aside, Perrini took her hand and pulled her into step with his ground-eating stride. Kimberley let him, because he was right, damn his arrogant, Italian-suited hide. Despite the speed with which he whisked her across the airport terminal, she could almost feel the hot breath of the pursuing media on her back.

This was neither the time nor the place for explanations. Inside his car, however, she would get answers.

Now that the initial shock had been blown away—by the haste of their retreat, by the heat of her gathering indignation, by the rush of adrenaline fired by Perrini's presence and the looming verbal battle—her brain was starting to tick over. This had to be her father's doing. And if it was a Howard Blackstone publicity ploy, then it had to be about Blackstone Diamonds, the company that ruled his life.

The knowledge made her chest tighten with a familiar ache of disillusionment.

She'd known her father would be flying in from Sydney for today's opening of the newest in his chain of exclusive, high-end jewelry boutiques. The opulent shop front sat adjacent to the rival business where Kimberley worked. No coincidence, she thought bitterly, just as it was no coincidence that Ric Perrini was here in Auckland ushering her to his car.

Perrini was Howard Blackstone's right-hand man, second in command at Blackstone Diamonds, a legacy of his short-lived marriage to the boss's daughter. No doubt her father had sent him to fetch her; the question was *why?*

* * * * *

When Kimberley Blackstone's father is
presumed dead, Kimberley is required to take
over the helm of Blackstone Diamonds. She
has to work closely with her ex, Ric Perrini, to
battle not only the press, but also the fierce
attraction still sizzling between them. Does Ric
feel the same...or is it the power her share of
Blackstone Diamonds will provide him as he
battles for boardroom supremacy.

Look for

VOWS &
A VENGEFUL GROOM
by
BRONWYN
JAMESON

Available January wherever you buy books

REQUEST YOUR FREE BOOKS!

Harlequin® Historical
Historical Romantic Adventure!

2 FREE NOVELS PLUS 2 FREE GIFTS!

YES! Please send me 2 FREE Harlequin® Historical novels and my 2 FREE gifts. After receiving them, if I don't wish to receive any more books, I can return the shipping statement marked "cancel." If I don't cancel, I will receive 6 brand-new novels every month and be billed just $4.69 per book in the U.S., or $5.24 per book in Canada, plus 25¢ shipping and handling per book and applicable taxes, if any*. That's a savings of close to 15% off the cover price! I understand that accepting the 2 free books and gifts places me under no obligation to buy anything. I can always return a shipment and cancel at any time. Even if I never buy another book from Harlequin, the two free books and gifts are mine to keep forever.

246 HDN EEWW   349 HDN EEW9

Name _____ (PLEASE PRINT) _____

Address _____ Apt. # _____

City _____ State/Prov. _____ Zip/Postal Code _____

Signature (if under 18, a parent or guardian must sign)

Mail to the **Harlequin Reader Service®:**
IN U.S.A.: P.O. Box 1867, Buffalo, NY 14240-1867
IN CANADA: P.O. Box 609, Fort Erie, Ontario L2A 5X3

Not valid to current Harlequin Historical subscribers.

Want to try two free books from another line?
Call 1-800-873-8635 or visit www.morefreebooks.com.

* Terms and prices subject to change without notice. NY residents add applicable sales tax. Canadian residents will be charged applicable provincial taxes and GST. This offer is limited to one order per household. All orders subject to approval. Credit or debit balances in a customer's account(s) may be offset by any other outstanding balance owed by or to the customer. Please allow 4 to 6 weeks for delivery.

Your Privacy: Harlequin is committed to protecting your privacy. Our Privacy Policy is available online at www.eHarlequin.com or upon request from the Reader Service. From time to time we make our lists of customers available to reputable firms who may have a product or service of interest to you. If you would prefer we not share your name and address, please check here. ☐

HH07

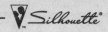

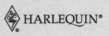

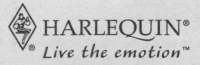

COMING NEXT MONTH FROM
HARLEQUIN®
HISTORICAL

- **THE VANISHING VISCOUNTESS**
  by **Diane Gaston**
  (Regency)
  When the Marquess of Tannerton rescues a beautiful stranger from
  a shipwreck, he has no idea that she is the notorious fugitive the
  Vanishing Viscountess! Can he prove her innocence—or will his fight
  to save her bring an English lord to the gallows?
  *RITA® Award winner Diane Gaston visits the gritty underworld of
  Regency life in this thrill-packed story!*

- **MAVERICK WILD**
  by **Stacey Kayne**
  (Western)
  The last thing war-hardened cowboy Chance Morgan needs is a
  reminder of the guilt and broken promises of his past. But when pretty
  Cora Mae arrives at his ranch, her sweetness soon begins to break down
  his defenses.
  *Warmly emotional, brilliantly evoking the Wild West, Stacey Kayne is an
  author to watch!*

- **ON THE WINGS OF LOVE**
  by **Elizabeth Lane**
  (Twentieth Century)
  Wealthy and spoiled, Alexandra Bromley wants an adventure. And
  when a handsome pilot crash-lands on her parents' lawn, she gets a lot
  more than she bargained for!
  *Join Elizabeth Lane as she explores America at the dawn of a new
  century!*

- **HER WARRIOR KING**
  by **Michelle Willingham**
  (Medieval)
  Behaving like a demure Norman lady does nothing except get Isabel
  married to a barbarian Irish king who steals her away on their wedding
  day. She refuses to be a proper wife to him—but Patrick MacEgan
  makes her blood race, and she's beginning to wonder how long she can
  hold out!
  *Don't miss this sexy Irish warrior—the third MacEgan brother to fight
  for the heart of his lady.*